NEW YORK REVIEW BOOKS
CLASSICS

THE ADVENTURES OF SINDBAD

GYULA KRÚDY (1878–1933) was born in Nyíregyháza in northeastern Hungary. His mother had been a maid for the aristocratic Krúdy family, and she and his father, a lawyer, did not marry until Gyula was seventeen. Krúdy began writing short stories and publishing brief newspaper pieces while still in his teens. Rebelling against his father's wish that he become a lawyer, he worked as a newspaper editor for several years before moving to Budapest, where he, his wife, and two children lived off the money he made as a writer of short stories. In 1911 he found success with *Sindbad's Youth*, the first of his books recounting the exploits of his fictional alter ego. Krúdy's subsequent novels about contemporary Budapest, including *The Crimson Coach* (1914) and *Sunflower* (1918; available from NYRB Classics), proved popular during the First World War and the Hungarian Revolution, but his drinking, gambling, and philandering left him broke and led to the dissolution of his first marriage. During the late 1920s and early 1930s, Krúdy suffered from declining health and a diminishing readership, even as he was awarded Hungary's most prestigious literary award, the Baumgarten Prize. Forgotten in the years after his death, Krúdy was rediscovered in 1940, when Sándor Márai published *Sindbad Comes Home*, a fictionalized account of Krúdy's last day. The success of the book led to a revival of Krúdy's works and to his recognition as one of the greatest Hungarian writers.

GEORGE SZIRTES is a Hungarian-born English poet and translator. He received the T. S. Eliot Prize for *Reel* (2004), and his *New and Collected Poems* were published in 2008. As a translator of poetry and fiction he has won a variety of prizes and awards, including the European Poetry Translation Prize and the Déry Prize.

THE ADVENTURES OF SINDBAD

GYULA KRÚDY

*Translated from the Hungarian and
with an introduction by*
GEORGE SZIRTES

NEW YORK REVIEW BOOKS

New York

THIS IS A NEW YORK REVIEW BOOK
PUBLISHED BY THE NEW YORK REVIEW OF BOOKS
IN ASSOCIATION WITH CENTRAL EUROPEAN CLASSICS

435 Hudson Street, New York, NY 10014
www.nyrb.com

First published in Hungarian as *Szindbád Három Könyve*, 1944
This translation first published in English by Central European University Press, 1998

The publishers would like to thank John E. Bowlt and The Vendome Press for their
assistance in acquiring the cover image for this volume.

Library of Congress Cataloging-in-Publication Data
Krúdy, Gyula.
[Szindbád English]
The adventures of Sindbad / by Gyula Krúdy ; translated and with an introduction
by George Szirtes.
      p. cm. — (Central European Classics [Budapest, Hungary])
Translation of: Szindbád.
Includes bibliographical references.
ISBN 978-1-59017-445-6 (alk. paper)
1. Sindbad the Sailor (Legendary character)—Fiction. I. Szirtes, George, 1948–
PH3281.K89S9513 2011
894'.511332—dc22

                              2011012601

ISBN 978-1-59017-445-6

Printed in the United States of America on acid-free paper.
10 9 8 7 6 5 4 3 2

Contents

Introduction

I‍t is a considerable achievement to have turned yourself into a literary cult, to have your name associated
not only with particular districts of your capital city
but with an entire mode of feeling. In Hungary, the
terms 'Krúdyesque' and 'the world of Krúdy' have a
currency which extends beyond books and conjures an
experience comprised of the nostalgic, the fantastic and
the ironic. It is even more remarkable that this experience should be conveyed in a literary style that
anticipates both 'stream of consciousness' modernism
and the magic realism of contemporary Latin American
writers. Krúdy's work, in other words, is both of its time
and outside it. It encapsulates a passing world of manners but turns it into illusion and establishes that illusion
as a form of sensibility. In so doing it accomplishes a
quiet revolution that opens the possibilities of narrative
without ever appearing unnatural.

Gyula Krúdy was born in 1878, in Nyíregyháza, one
of the bigger towns in eastern Hungary at the foot of the
Carpathian mountains. The name of the town suggests
birches (*nyír* means birch) and the whole area is known
as the birch country. Krúdy's family was Catholic, and
his father, a lawyer, was a member of the local minor

gentry. The author was born in the old family house, but the household wasn't entirely conventional as his father lived with a common-law wife whom he married only at the end of his life. (His grandfather, a notable combatant in the 1848 revolution had himself been something of a libertine.) For four generations one son in the family had always been christened Gyula.

Krúdy wasn't particularly good at school. Like Sindbad, the hero of this book, he was educated in the Piarist establishment at Podolin, originally in Hungary, but then absorbed into Slovakia following the First World War. He started writing at an early age, and his first short story was accepted by the local paper when he was only thirteen. Within three years he had written some hundred stories.

Still in his teens, he ran away from home and sought work with the journals of the larger towns of eastern Hungary and Transylvania – at that time also part of Hungary. His father disinherited him and he lived from hand to mouth – a gambler, drinker, womaniser, bon viveur and occasional duellist. He was not quite eighteen when he arrived in Budapest in 1896. The date is significant for it supposedly marked one thousand years of Magyar settlement in the Carpathian basin and the founding of the Hungarian state. A world fair was arranged to commemorate this millennium. Since 1867 Budapest had been the fastest growing city in Europe and the Millennial Fair, with its blending of historical pageant and technological progress, marked the apex of this development. The world's second underground railway system – the first was in London – was opened in Budapest in 1896. Europe's largest stock exchange had been finished in Budapest the previous year and the Hungarian Parliament, the largest parliament building in the world at that time, was close to completion. Hungary had modern art and modern literature, an active commercial sector and a busy cosmopolitan culture. It had theatre, opera and its own national literary epics.

When Krúdy first moved to Budapest he had intended to be a poet but no poems were forthcoming; stories and journalism took all his attention. Handsome and charismatic, at the age of twenty he married a Jewish writer and schoolteacher called Bella Spiegler who wrote under the pseudonym of 'Satanella'. By that time his first volume of stories had been published and he was writing for most of the major journals and periodicals of Budapest. Bella was older than him by some years and bore him four children, though marriage for Krúdy was a far from stable domestic arrangement. He lived on credit and advances and was rarely at home; people – especially women – fell in love with him and were happy to support him.

All this makes Krúdy sound like just another of those playboy-scribblers of the *fin de siècle.* In England he might have fallen off a bar stool like Lionel Johnson, and that would have been the end of him. But Krúdy was not of the Celtic Twilight temperament and his writing, though ornate, complex and aesthetic, was far more robust and individual. At its best it was recognised as an extraordinary enterprise which established not only a style but a heightened sensuous world, a Hungary of the imagination that Hungarians found both seductive and recognisable. This world encompassed both the provinces from which he came and Budapest.

The historian John Lukács observes that there was something rakish and romantic about the sexual life of the capital. Women outnumbered men. There were many high-class brothels, gambling dens, casinos, races and other amusements. Assignations in the Biedermeyer apartments of Pest, on the commercial left bank of the Danube, might be discreet but they were certainly not uncommon. There were fine cheap restaurants, cafés where writers and lovers were welcome, with live gypsy bands on hand to entertain them.

In many ways Hungary was still a feudal society. Out in the country, where Krúdy was born, peasants were tied to the service of the great landlords and conditions were harsh. Austria regarded the whole of Hungary as a sleepy, potentially barbaric province with one foot in modern Europe, the other in the Near East. The Hungarians formed a linguistic and ethnic minority in the dual monarchy led by Austria, but Hungary had many ethnic minorities of its own: Romanians and Slovaks, as well as Gypsies. Its territory was three times the size of current Hungary and extended from the Carpathians through the great plains of the central basin to the Adriatic seaboard with its port of Fiume – now Rijeka, in Slovenia. The impoverished minor nobility lived in country residences and small towns, maintaining as much of their manners as remained possible under the circumstances. The old hierarchies were largely observed and codes of courtesy deeply valued.

The Sindbad stories, which both reflected and under-
mined these values, appeared in magazines and individual volumes between 1911 and 1917. By 1919 Sindbad's Hungary was dead. Defeat in the First World War
brought the dream-world to an end. In 1918, following
that defeat, and the so-called Autumn Roses Revolution, a liberal–socialist coalition under Count Mihály
Károlyi assumed control. Within a few months it had
been ousted by the Communist Béla Kun and his Republic of Councils. Amid the chaos, to the incredulity
of most Hungarians, the backward Romanian forces
marched in, defeated the Hungarian Red Army and
ransacked Budapest. This was an extraordinary trauma
for the nation. When the Romanians withdrew, under
allied pressure, it was only for the rightist forces of
Admiral Horthy to take over. Horthy rode into Budapest
on a white horse. Reprisals followed and many left-
wing writers and politicians fled into exile. Krúdy, who
had very little time for politics, was briefly in trouble
because of some articles he had written defending the
Republic of Councils.

For his country, worse was to follow: under the terms
of the Treaties of Versailles and Trianon the Austro-
Hungarian Empire was broken up and the countries on
Hungary's borders, whose nationals made up most of
Hungary's ethnic minorities, were rewarded for their
support of the *entente* with vast new tracts of land.
Transylvania, so central to Hungarian history and containing some of the oldest Hungarian settlements, was
given over to Romania; Pozsony, once capital of Hungary, was renamed Bratislava and is today the capital of

Slovakia. Vast swathes of greater Hungary were swallowed up by Yugoslavia. Hungary lost one third of its population as well as two thirds of its territory. The world of Sindbad was truly finished: the country through which Sindbad had roamed was now relegated to works of fiction.

By the time he died in 1933 Krúdy had produced over fifty novels, some three thousand short stories, over a thousand articles and sketches and seven plays for the stage. As regards Krúdy's fiction, his prose style is highly original. The nineteenth-century novelist Kálmán Mikszáth might be cited as an early influence but Mikszáth was a realist, as was the other major novelist of the time, Mór Jókai, and Krúdy's bent was not for social realism but for a range of complex moods arising out of a state of melancholy. A highly literary kind of melancholy can be found in the Symbolist writers of the period. Sindbad himself is frequently in a melancholic condition, he listens to gypsy music, he watches the autumnal leaves swirl at his feet, hears the distant hoot of the train, the lapping of the river and admires the swirling of fog. He watches young skin dry and develop crow's-feet, he watches his own hair turn silver. A rich strain of late nineteenth-century melancholy accompanies everything he thinks or does. At times the language seems doom-laden and over-ripe, over-repetitive in its use of 'little', 'sad', and, inevitably, 'melancholy' itself.

But the remarkable thing is that, for all its period melancholy, *Sindbad* is a modernist work. Like Prufrock, Sindbad has measured out his life with coffee spoons and walked amongst the lowest of the dead – in fact, for much of the book he *is* dead, a walking sentient ghost musing upon his own ghostliness – yet all the time the subversive force of irony is breaking things up, infusing the elegiac sadness with a welcome disruptive energy. In doing so it prefigures the stream of consciousness explored by Proust, Woolf and Joyce: an interesting point of correspondence with Joyce appears when Sindbad advises one of his lovers, 'Monkey', to read the works of Paul de Kock, a writer of erotic stories equally appreciated by Molly Bloom. Most remarkably, it anticipates the magic realism of Gabriel García Márquez and Isabel Allende.

The Sindbad stories refer to real and possible metamorphoses: at one point Sindbad changes into a sprig of mistletoe and contemplates turning into a comb. This sense of shift is reflected in Krúdy's syntax – something strange begins to happen to language and its relation to experience. Krúdy's long rolling sentences are held together by sentiment, sensuality and dream, but for all their sense of gentle flux, something is breaking them up. They are open-ended affairs which begin in the ordinary way but fly off at specific points of association, constantly diverting the reader away from the linear syntactic flow of the narrative. Tenses change continually. The subject–verb–object structure is subverted, in much the same way as a hierarchy or social order might be, from within. Before the reader knows it, the language has come to pieces in his hands, leaving a curiously sweet erotic vacuum, like an ache without a centre. That ache is at the heart of Krúdy's prose and particularly of the Sindbad stories.

It may be fanciful to see the breaking up of Hungary anticipated in the breaking up of Krúdy's prose but it is tempting. There is something prophetic about the way the fiction works. It looks resolutely backwards for its ethos – Sindbad is, after all, over three hundred years old, if he is any age at all – and the effort of having to move the narrative forwards simply splinters the syntactic structure. If the prophetic power of literature lies in the imagination's helpless sensitivity to currents of change, then Krúdy's fiction is an outstanding illustration of that power. The elegant barque of his prose has already struck the rocks and every wave sends a few more beams and planks shivering into the water.

The very first paragraph of 'Youth', the first story in the book, serves as a model for what is to follow:

> Once upon a damp and moonlit night a man with greying hair was watching the autumn mist form figures of chimney-sweeps on the rooftops. Somewhere in the monastery at Podolin, he was thinking, there is, or was, an old painting, showing a shaggy-haired figure with a wild upcurled moustache, a thick beard, red as a woman's hair, two big round eyes with elongated pale blue pupils and a complexion as ruddy as the colour on a white tablecloth when light passes through a full wine glass on a sunny winter noon. This man was Prince Lubomirski.

Introduction

The time is uncertain, the view mistily retrospective but the place is precise and the vision highly detailed. Chimney-sweeps appear then disappear along with the mist. The object of focus is not real life but a painting. As we look at the painting and note the wild ancestral figure we stare into his eyes and discover a beam of light passing through a wine glass on a white tablecloth on a sunny winter noon. Then the figure is named and we read seven paragraphs about him and his times before getting to the subject of the story which concerns an incident from Sindbad's childhood – though we must remember it is the man with greying hair who is recalling it. The action of the story amounts to no more than a brief tragic anecdote about the death by drowning of a boy nicknamed Pope Gregory, an anecdote told lightly enough but constantly moving between light and darkness, hinting at the possibility of romance.

Prince Lubomirski, who does not appear to be an agent in the story, is an important symbolic figure, a seducer and ever-fertile father, the atavistic god to whom maidens are sacrificed. Róza, one of three sisters, and the romantic interest, is herself a kind of river goddess, who must be appeased, in her case with the unfortunate victim of the drowning. Prince Lubomirski and Róza are part of the landscape: they are emanations of the soil but are handled lightly, almost humorously. The manner of address is playful, presenting the incident as a sad funny story with a haunting erotic edge of sensuality. That haunting erotic edge is Sindbad's medium: it is the god Krúdy serves.

The adventures of Sindbad consist of nothing but interrupted, extended, inconclusive anecdotes whose purpose is to conjure the god, not to satisfy notions of character and consequence. In this sense they are amoral. The drowning in the first story may be read as a highly unfair punishment for Pope Gregory's unattractiveness: the boy's hunch-back invites rejection by the god's female aspect. But there is no time to pity Pope Gregory – now you see him, now you don't and that is all there is to it. The story of the drowning is not the real issue, it is merely the occasion. Even when Krúdy embarks on a longer tale there is no real narrative consequence. One thing happens, then another, but ostensible events are mostly occasions for the hidden 'real' event, which is the death and resurrection of desire. Desire is the appropriate word. To call it love would be premature. Fidelity is what partners demand of each other, not what they grant. They feel intensely but their feelings are shallow and this does not bother them. Krúdy's characters find the lightness of their being wholly bearable.

So the narrative line is broken time and again, and Sindbad dies and returns and drifts through time as if time itself were nothing but an autumn mist. Neither is he restricted to a merely human existence. He can turn into inanimate objects. He is protean in so far as desire is so, being able to read himself into any body or any thing. There is a hint of the late Byron of *Don Juan* and *Beppo* in the way Sindbad floats. Sindbad is a sort of sentimental digressive Don Juan, and his world is not unlike that of Byron's Venice – more provincial of course, its glamour second-hand and peripheral, but genuine for all that. In Krúdy, Hungary becomes a floating world, much like Byron's.

That sense of the periphery relates to the notion of empire too. The standard imperial values are reduced to resonances and associations vainly flapping in the provincial void. Of what value is the pioneer spirit, the spirit of enterprise, buccaneering courage or high-minded philanthropy here? Here, opportunities for advancement are chiefly in the form of reverie, a reverie whose relation to the possible and here-and-now is problematic. The reality on which fantasy must work is itself fading. Krúdy loves everything faded. The whole paraphernalia of the Austro-Hungarian pastoral has begun to look slightly ridiculous to a sharp eye. Krúdy knows the game is up, that the world awaiting Sindbad's descendants will not be like that of Sindbad's own centuries. In 'Sindbad and the Actress' he shows us that which had appeared to be eternal in the Hungarian village.

> The people changed but they were replaced by others precisely like them. As if birth, death and marriage were all part of some curious joke. Even now it was the ancestral dead sitting round the table. They reproduced themselves: women, children. The weathercock spins, the wind and rain beat at the roof precisely as before, and neither the cloud approaching from the west nor the meadow stretching far into the distance appears to acknowledge the

fact that the man sitting at the window is of this century not the last.

Portraits of ancestors appear throughout the adventures. They add tone to that mortuary charm. The irony underlying them proclaims the fact that Sindbad does not fully believe in either them or himself. He is an aging lover and has already died several times over. Those magical transformations and that continual shifting between spirit and flesh only go to show that he is hardly there.

He is certainly a creature of vestiges. Sindbad is a self-proclaimed voyeur and fetishist. He loves women's clothes almost more than the women themselves. He admits that he finds the naked woman disappointing. He has an eye for fashion and enjoys watching women parade in their latest outfits. In 'Sindbad's Dream' he notes women in their silken dresses 'which they raised to reveal high white-laced boots'; in 'Winter Journey' we meet the woman of his dreams 'still standing on the threshold in her lacquered ankle boots and delicate silk stockings'. 'Your figure is as it was, neat and graceful,' Sindbad says to one of his many actress loves, Paula, in another story. 'Let me smell your hair! Show me your shoes and your stockings! You ought to wear finer gloves. The little ribbon about your neck is charming.' He is equally fastidious about the details of men's clothing, preferring the slightly romantic and faintly ridiculous, though he knows the difference between them. In 'The Woman Who Told Tales', young Albert, who has been deeply smitten by the mysterious siren and ex-flower girl, Mrs Boldogfalvi, wears a highly romantic costume of tall riding boots, cloak and a plumed hat. In fact he is not unlike Sindbad himself when Mrs Boldogfalvi first meets him. Pursuing Mrs Boldogfalvi, who has grown bored with him, Albert arrives at the inn she has just left, his face covered in dust, throws down his plumed hat and cries: 'Devil take her! What am I doing wearing this fancy dress?'

Fancy dress is an important element of Sindbad's fantasies. Take a passage from another of Krúdy's winding sentences:

> … when behind open windows striking women of foreign appearance are taking their clothes off in the sleeping compartments and men wearing military decorations are reading broadsheets in the dining car, and you pick up that blend of Havana and cologne even through the smell of coaldust, then Sindbad becomes a black moustached, Henry VIII-bearded sleeping car attendant in a gold braided hat, who calmly and elegantly steps into the sleeping compartments, approaches the lovely Romanian woman who is already dozing and asks, in a cool but delicate manner, 'Is there anything else I could get you, madam?'

Here, as elsewhere, Sindbad is a little Oedipal boy sensually pleasing his mother. The wisest and most fully rounded of Krúdy's female protagonists is the woman nicknamed Monkey, who, in only the second story of the book, is already left to arrange matters after Sindbad's death. She raises his chin to the light of the window, closely examines his face, strokes his hair and says to him:

> '... sometimes I love you so much I feel less like your lover – your discarded, abandoned and forgotten lover – than like your mother. I know you so well. It is as if I had given birth to you.'

This is one of the key perceptions of the book, not so much for its revelation about missing mothers or the lure of the maternal but for its recognition of Sindbad's ambivalence. It turns out that Monkey knows more about his life than he does. A simplistic reading would suggest that all the women in Sindbad's life are merely projections of his desire, but Sindbad himself feels and acts as though he were a projection of theirs. Sindbad's contemplations on women will sometimes appear offensive to a modern reader. The passage in 'An Overnight Stay', where we are told that Sindbad likes 'Leaves in the park in autumn, blotched as if with blood, and abandoned windmills where one day he might murder the woman he loved best' is worrying, and another in 'Escape from Women', where Sindbad suggests that treating women like children is downright insulting. But the very same passage later transforms these child-women into would-be mothers of Sindbad. As the ruminations progress, Sindbad comes to recognise himself as a rogue, one who, in the Middle Ages, 'would have gone the rounds of the prisons where he would have been shorn, first of his nose, then of his ears'. This is familiar territory of course, and is only half-heartedly offered as an excuse.

In a paper recently given at the Collegium in Budapest, the translator John Bátki pointed out how Krúdy evokes the old Goddess cults of his home country, the marshy wetlands of the River Tisza. Bátki draws on research by Marija Gimbutas into the neolithic religions of old Europe to demonstrate that Krúdy's later work is open to anthropological readings. Perhaps Sindbad is a faded Adonis or Tammuz. Even if that is the case, we simply cannot take him at his own evaluation. Krúdy doesn't, nor, for that matter, does Sindbad himself. Sindbad says he cannot help but tell the truth, but this truth concerns his condition, not any objective state of affairs. The condition subsumes his hypocrisy.

> 'He could never forgive women. He thought he perceived miraculous qualities in them, a combination of the fidelity of the saints with the virtues of the martyrs. And how he would rage when one of them took up with another man though it was he who had long left her.'

Hypocrisy *is* the state of affairs in dreams. Sindbad acts ironically in a world in which he half-believes. In so far as he believes in it, we are given to understand that he is naïve – a creature of the past. Sindbad's dreams are clearly historical fancies – tiny costumed tableaux, doll's house flirtations – but the women's dreams are all the more substantial for including him as he is. In effect he is validated by their dreams.

Dreams are the ultimate channel of communication. 'I dreamt you were dreaming with me, so I set out,' he says to Paula on meeting her. In their dreams he revisits the women he once seduced, or who seduced him – or else returns as a ghost. They lock him in secret rooms. They want to take him away to their quiet country retreats. He is what they would have him be. 'His whole long life he had been "my darling" to two or three women at a time,' Krúdy tells us. Maybe this is because Sindbad has 'a genius for observing women, for secretly following them and discovering their hopes, secrets and desires'. He is a beautiful boy-child with a grey moustache and perfect manners, the infant fascinated by the female principle and its power. And indeed, as an exercise in power, it is hard to say who is in control. Women kill themselves for him, but he kills himself for them too. They have him on a string as much as he has them. It is the mutual exercise of erotic power that makes the transaction such a pleasure.

Yet the pleasure is never free of danger and there is usually a price to be paid for it. Pope Gregory pays it. So do the dead babies sleeping in the ditch, those 'tiny souls who had perished downless, featherless' but who nevertheless resurrect themselves as little frogs and hop onto their mothers' feet as the women are crossing for sexual assignations in the graveyard. So do the suicides drifting in the waters of the Danube and the dead mother who hears her own daughter being seduced by a ghost directly above her grave – all pay the price. Time and again Sindbad envisages his own death although it frightens him. When his lover Fanny proposes a suicide pact he finds the thought so terrifying that he shudders: 'I know death. Death is for women.' But it is he who has been dead through most of the book. In any case, the idea of the suicide pact has come to the lady a few hours too late. It is already dawn. 'The milkman is due,' says Fanny, 'my husband will arrive by the first train, the servants will be up and ready to go to the market ... and I shall go to hospital to visit my sick brother.'

Romance requires night and mists. Clear light destroys it. A young Hungarian man of the 1920s might have used Sindbad as a working manual of sexual relations. He might not have suspected the tricks those strange long open sentences were playing on him; that the carpet was, in effect, being pulled from under his and the author's own feet. Yet the manual still has its surprises. The vampirical Sindbad is less interested in the blood of young virgins than in the nourishment provided by fellow veterans of the sexual campaign.

Once, when an officer of the Hussars insulted him, Krúdy tore the man's sword from his waist and presented the sword to the madam of a brothel. He then fought the duel to which the Hussar had challenged him – and won. He would sit up all night drinking. On another occasion, thinking that Krúdy had fallen asleep, an exhausted drinking companion tried to tip-toe from the room. 'Come back and talk some more,' Krúdy's deep voice ordered him.

The voice that speaks to us in *The Adventures of Sindbad* has authority. Its discourse is woven out of the night-talk of duels and seductions remembered but not quite believed. 'Let us therefore close the file on Sindbad's not altogether pointless and occasionally amusing existence,' Krúdy declares in 'Escape from Women', dismissing his romantic ironical hero with an equally ironic gesture. The new world is moving under Sindbad much as the underground train moved under the feet of the citizens of Budapest, shaking the cobbles of the old.

George Szirtes

THE ADVENTURES OF
SINDBAD

Youth

———

Once upon a damp and moonlit night a man with greying hair was watching the autumn mist form figures of chimney-sweeps on the rooftops. Somewhere in the monastery at Podolin, he was thinking, there is, or was, an old painting, showing a shaggy-haired figure with a wild upcurled moustache, a thick beard, red as a woman's hair, two big round eyes with elongated pale blue pupils, and a complexion as ruddy as the colour on a white tablecloth when light passes through a full wine glass on a sunny winter noon. This man was Prince Lubomirski.

Who he was,* what kind of man, before he found himself among other worn gilt frames in the old monastery, is not strictly relevant to this tale. Suffice it to say he was there on the wall, beneath the vault, where peeling plaster revealed faint traces of a mural of long dead saints amusing themselves. St Anne was seated on a low stool, her face somewhat drained of colour by this time, only her two bleary eyes still staring enquiringly at the students who clattered down the cobbled passageway in their heavy boots. The good woman was eternally solicitous about their education. St George, mean-

1

while, was busily killing his dragon – and Prince Lubomirski took his place in the middle.

The monastery had its share of non-paying novices, and their stout tutors were always ready to terrify them with those big round eyes. The prince had, in his day, supported the propagation of piety by contributing some fine round cobbles to the fabric of the building, so even after his death he retained a certain interest in the disciplining of errant students. Poor Slovakian boys who had found themselves transported directly from tall pine forests to the thick walls of the monastery, raised their caps respectfully to his wine red complexion.

The young ladies of Podolin who came to the monks for absolution would wreathe his picture with flowers fresh from the meadow, and women, who a couple of centuries before would have given birth to red-bearded, shaggy-haired children, prayed before the prince's image precisely as they did before pictures of the saints. (To be sure, they had forgotten how some two centuries ago, the prince would delightedly remove his buffalo skin gloves in the presence of ladies kneeling at his feet. But he was long past removing his gloves now.)

In this manner Lubomirski remained lord of the manor well after his death: local boys were inevitably christened George, and each Sunday before the town hall the local dignitaries would let off a rocket in honour both of the Lord and of George Lubomirski. (True, they used only half as much gunpowder for the latter.)

The gentleman with greying hair, who, seated one night at his writing table, recalled that vaulted corridor where the heels of the novices clattered and echoed, then faded away in the distance, had himself been a student at the monastery and knew the district well. His name was Sindbad. He had selected this name from his favourite book of stories, *The Thousand and One Nights,* for in those days, it was still fairly common for knight errants, poets, actors and passionate scholars to choose names for themselves. One hunchbacked lad had chosen to be addressed as Gregory, after the pope, heaven knows why.

Sindbad respected Prince Lubomirski, but he raised his hat to him in much the same way as he did to the stationer, Müller, whose little shop was situated in the shadow of a gateway and was therefore always dark. Here, in this gloom, nature worked in reverse, for while old man Müller had no moustache, his saucy raven-haired daughter, Fanni, did. For a long time Fanni was embarrassed by this, but one day a young teacher arrived in town, and he told her the moustache was both lovely and seductive. And Fanni was seized by such great happiness on hearing this that she leapt into the River Poprád near the dam.

Sindbad's parents, let it be known, were punctilious in paying his fees to the monastery and on more than one occasion sent barrels of wine as a contribution to Holy Communion, over which Sindbad officiated, wearing his red surplice and rattling off the Confiteor at the speed of light, before ceremoniously and becomingly ringing his bell, as if the novices in the rear pews were only waiting for this word of command before they could get down on their knees. It was in this office one Sunday, while wearing his red surplice, that he succeeded in seducing Anna Kacskó, who had come to mass along with a few friends of hers. How did all this happen?

One reason why Sindbad neglected to thank the prince in an appropriately humble fashion was because he was a boarding student at the Kacskó residence. Old man Kacskó was a chief magistrate – one of the 'old school' you used to be able to find in little hillside towns. In his youth he might have been no more than a magistrate's runner, then a magistrate's clerk; but as time went on he grew a beard and learned the ropes simply by being there. And as his beard grew so did his belly, until, in the end, he became chief magistrate. There is nothing in the highland magistrates of that rakish quality typical of the lowland sort; they are solid upright men who have big families and do their bit at home cutting up wood and making candles, rarely losing their tempers unless the cook burns the soup. Old man Kacskó brought his heavy fist down on the table.

'I am chief magistrate!' he thundered.

Minka, his gentle, glum, neatly combed wife answered as was her wont, 'Yes, but not when you're at home.'

'How dare you talk like that to me in front of my daughters?' shouted old man Kacskó, and put his hand to his ear as if trying to catch the words of some Slovakian plaintiff at a hearing.

'They are *my* daughters,' Minka sighed. 'The chief magistrate shows little interest in the fact that they should be married one day.'

After this there was little left for Gyula Kacskó, chief magistrate, to do but escape to his office. He sent one of his clerks home to fetch his favourite pipe.

It was true that no one seemed to care much whether the Kacskó girls married or not. There were three of them, three maidens, brought up to be pretty, healthy and strapping, and they lived, as did Sindbad, on the upper floors of the house. They took weekly turns to do the cooking: Magda excelled at mutton, Anna at cabbage and Róza at sweet pastries. In the afternoon or the evening, when Sindbad had, for his own good reasons, to leave the downstairs sitting room (if only so that old man Kacskó and mother Minka should be able to have a proper row without the chief magistrate escaping to his office), the young ladies took turns to escort Sindbad, who was frightened of being alone and was not too fond of study, to his room, to sit at his desk, engage in a little handiwork and read endless novels. Magda and Anna were usually so absorbed in their novels that Sindbad could fall asleep over his homework without them noticing. But Róza, who was just sixteen, and was not as likely as the others to look condescendingly on the adolescent Sindbad, would often reach over, grab a hank of the student's thick dark hair in her fair hands, and give it a sound, good-humoured tug. The boy yelped in pain. Róza blushed all the deeper and tugged even harder.

'Study!' she cried, her eyes sparkling, 'or else, as God is my witness, Lubomirski will fail you.'

Sindbad quickly bent over his book again, till one day on the deserted upper floor, where bags of oats lay like dead men in the empty rooms, a sudden wind sprung up. Róza was frightened and shut her eyes listening to its roar, then, perhaps because the fear grew stronger in her, she gave a little shiver and leant against the boy, pale and distraught, letting her head drop onto his shoulder and putting her arm about his neck.

As for Sindbad, the wind gave him such a fright he didn't dare turn the page of his book though he had learned all that was to be learned from the one that lay open before him.

So, back in the days when George Lubomirski watched over the progress of the pupils of Podolin, grasping, in his buffalo skin gloves, the hilt of his sword on which representations of the currently popular saints were clearly to be seen – in the days when Róza Kacskó good-humouredly, energetically and somewhat tenderly tugged Sindbad's hair, then leaned her head upon his shoulder once the punishment had been duly administered, there was a boy who was second to none in his study of theology, of the sacraments and of the piety due to icons, who for one reason or other was referred to as Pope Gregory by the novices of the ancient monastery. Pope Gregory was a hunchbacked little boy with features as delicate as the holy wafer he received once a week. Though Sindbad often took the opportunity of punching Pope Gregory, he nevertheless made friends with him, and what's more, one afternoon, just when Róza was due to be sitting at his desk at the Kacskós', supervising his studies, he invited the little hunchback up. It could only have been to show off Róza, to demonstrate her friendship, her lovely eyes and fair hands.

This is how the visit of Pope Gregory went: Róza remained serious and silent the whole time, behaved condescendingly to both boys and was not at all willing to tug Sindbad's hair, though she had never wasted an opportunity to do so in the past.

And far from resting her head on Sindbad's shoulders, or putting her arms about his neck, she railed at him violently. 'I wonder that Lubomirski tolerates such a hopeless student at the monastery!'

Poor hunchbacked Pope Gregory gawped as if bewitched by the sight of the jerkin tightening on Róza's naked arms and the pearly buttons heaving silently on her rounded bosom.

But Róza mocked him and slapped him on the back, crying, 'Just look at this boy. He has a hump like a camel.'

Pope Gregory blinked, his face quietly reddened and he left the upper floor with tears in his eyes.

Sindbad felt a certain bitterness that evening when Róza affectionately rumpled his hair, laid her ashen face against his, grasped his shoulder firmly and swung on the chair. He kept seeing the hunchback's tearful face and concentrated as firmly as he could on his studies, if only to annoy Róza.

'Really, what do you see in that toad?' Róza asked, annoyed when Sindbad refused to take his eyes from the book.

He stretched, stood up and stepped lazily over to the window. The evening – a mild June evening – brought to his ear the mingled noises of travellers on the road snaking up the little hill. The first stars were peering over the distant mountains like children playing at hide-and-seek.

'From now on you can study with the hunchbacked toad,' said Róza later, quite solemnly. 'Teach yourself Latin, if you like him so much.'

This mild cloud was the reason that Sindbad went bathing with Pope Gregory in the River Poprád the following afternoon, behaving as if they were the best of friends. The Poprád wound between timber barriers under the ancient monastery, dark and silent as a lake. Further out, in the middle of the current, the waves danced and frothed as merrily as if they had learned the art of cheerful travelling from merchants trafficking up and down the hills, whistling, singing, tippling their way from country to country.

Naturally, the boys bathed in the deep still water, holding on to the iron staples in the timber, dangling their legs in the bottomless pool. The little hunchback felt absolutely safe in the company of the brave and admirable Sindbad. Suddenly he gave a triumphant cry, 'Hey, I can feel the river bed here!' He extended his thin legs. His inky fingers let go of the metal bar and the water silently closed over him. For a brief second Sindbad could still see the curious hump on his back under the surface of the river, then the water, the shore and the tall limes nearby grew unaccountably quiet as if the monastery had touched them with a magic wand and they had died on the spot, as in *The Thousand and One Nights.*

Sindbad leapt out of the water as if a crab had pinched him. He stared at the unmoving water and stirred it with a broken branch, then quickly snatched up his clothes. Tight-lipped and silent, he started to run towards the wooden bridge that straddled the Poprád like a great long-legged spider. He brushed against people who shook their heads at the pale little boy in full flight. Sindbad seemed to hear them muttering the name of the mysterious Lubomirski.

A boat was tied up at the bridge. His knife was sharp for he had little to do in his free time but sharpen it. It took but a moment to cut the rope. Meanwhile the strong current was already sweeping him downstream. Sindbad's eyes widened as he stared at the tall lime trees. Perhaps Pope Gregory the hunchback was still swinging there and the whole thing was merely a bad joke ...

But the place where the river lay dreaming was as silent as it had been a few moments ago. Carefully, Sindbad manoeuvred the boat to the spot where Pope Gregory had disappeared and poked an oar into the water as deep as it would go. Then he felt around with his arms in case Pope Gregory was just a few inches away ... Eventually he began to row quietly down river. He stopped now and then; the oar touched the pebbly bed of the shallow Poprád, a few larger stones emerged in the distance in deeper water like so many Pope Gregories, a scarlet trout shot by, terrified, and the river sparkled and foamed like liquid silver filtered through an enormous sieve.

The brickworks of the monastery slowly receded into the distance, yellow and red fruit trees extended along the bank, and Mr Privánka, one of the teachers, was doing a spot of weeding in the vegetable garden wearing heavy boots, his cassock rolled up. Sindbad flattened himself on the floor of boat for fear that he should see him. So he rowed on, leaving the monastery far behind. Boughs bent over the stream but there was nothing beneath them but a rotten old pine beam.

It was late afternoon by now, the sun was disappearing behind the mountains, and bare, abandoned fields stretched out ready for sleep on either side of the river. The silver Poprád no longer sparkled so brightly, a long lilac shadow was slowly settling across its reflective surface.

Then, some way down, midstream, he caught sight of the hunchback Pope Gregory, drifting face up in the spume. His two arms were extended either side of him, his mouth opened like a black hole. His legs were lost in the water.

Sindbad wiped his sweating brow and, for the first time, fully understood what had happened. The hunchback had drowned and he would get the blame. The image of Lubomirski would finally step out of the frame, in fact, he was already advancing on him with his red beard. Somewhere in the far distance Róza was standing under the dark boughs of the further shore, her hands joined behind her back, morosely, furiously glaring at the stars as she had done the night before ... The river seemed deep, mysterious and terrifying as he rowed after the corpse. Eventually he managed to catch hold of the hunchback Gregory's feet and, weeping and whimpering, he succeeded in hauling him into the boat.

He turned the boat round and slowly, wearily rowed back up the river.

Some time later Sindbad woke up at home and in bed.

The yellow lamp illuminated Róza's ashen face. The girl concentrated her enormous sparkling grey eyes on him and her lips whispered close into his ear. 'You are a brave boy. And I will love you for ever now.'

Sindbad's Dream

Once Sindbad dreamt he was a king in the heyday of Old England, a young king, about eighteen years old, wearing soft pointed shoes and a silken tunic. His hair was long and fell in waves. His eyes sparkled, he laughed a great deal, beautiful gold coins slipped from his fingers and he conversed in cheerful ringing tones. In this dream he was not only young but light-hearted, happy and magnificent, a soul conceived at sunrise. Courtiers perambulated around him on the grand terrace in costumes of Henry VII's time and the ladies had long trains to their silken dresses, which they raised to reveal high, white-laced boots. They nodded their curly heads to him when they passed. He continued seeing their white stockings a long time after the 'king' dream was over, even as he woke and moved his tired limbs one at a time. A whole row of white-stockinged female legs remained with him. And that morning, while he examined his deathly pale features in the mirror, he mused a little on the sensation of having been a young king during the night. Finally it occured to him that since he had experienced everything there was to be experienced in the world, he would probably die soon.

Sindbad's Dream

That day – a fine early autumn day – Sindbad dressed as carefully as befitted a man over three hundred years old. He selected a light-coloured tie and brightly polished shoes. The barber tucked Sindbad's head under his arm while he was shaving him, in the eastern manner, then rubbed scented oil into his grey hair. So prepared, old Sindbad set out to find the woman who had once worn white stockings and nodded to him when they met, addressing him as, 'My darling, my prince'. Sindbad would make a dismissive gesture, as if to say, 'Come now, enough of such nonsense.' Of course, that was back in the days when it was the common thing for women in the Buda Tunnel, in Krisztinaváros, in the Castle District, and indeed all the suburbs and environs of the capital, to address him as 'my darling'. His whole long life he had been 'my darling' to two or three women at any one time. He wouldn't leave a woman in peace until she had fallen in love with him. And that was why he had spent one tenth of his life waiting under windows, gazing longingly, humbly, unhappily or threateningly. He had a genius for observing women, for following them secretly and discovering their hopes, secrets and desires. Sindbad spent so much time standing motionless, listening to the whirring of sewing machines in small suburban houses, or taking a carriage in order to follow another carriage that galloped along bearing a sweet-scented woman in a wide hat, or stealthily watching a lace-curtained window lit up for the night, or observing a woman at prayer in the church and trying to guess who or what she might be praying for, that sometimes he barely had time to pluck the fruit he coveted. He tired of the business: some new adventure attracted him, excited his blood, his dreams, his appetite, so he failed to complete his previous mission. And thus it was that in the course of his life some eleven or twelve women waited for him in vain, at rendezvous, in closed carriages, on walks through woods or at distant stations where two trains should have met. Sindbad wasn't on the train, and the woman, that special one, would be standing hopefully at the window, watching from behind the curtains, frightened, wetting her dry lips with her tongue. And several trains would rattle by … including the train carrying the white-stockinged woman, the very one who, both in her letters and in person, addressed him as 'my darling', and there was nothing unusual in this at the time.

This woman was a widow known as 'Monkey' to all those who had loved her. She was a serious, decisive woman of great firmness of mind, for women usually change their pet names together with their admirers. She, however, remained Monkey right to the end. She hardly ever laughed, she never winked and she gazed at Sindbad with a desperate intensity when she threatened to cut her throat with an open razor because of him. She loved Sindbad with an absolute passion, as if he were her destiny. She couldn't stop loving him even years after Sindbad left her. She had been both deaf and blind until she was ten years old and believed it was this that made her think differently from other women. 'I will love my prince as long as I live. Whether I see him or not,' she told Sindbad on one of their infrequent meetings. 'Why must you love so foolishly?' Sindbad shrugged. 'There are other things in life besides love.'

Nevertheless, that day when forebodings of his own death surprised Sindbad, when he wanted to take his leave of all those women he still respected, he immediately thought of Monkey. The other women, the dark ones, fair ones, the young, the mature, the plump and the skinny, who had all planted their fatal loves in his heart, after whom he had run out of breath, sad, puzzled and perfectly willing to sacrifice his own life a hundred times over on their unresponsive behalf – all were neglected this day. He did not despise them but the thought of them no longer stirred his blood; the memory of their lips which still clung to his lips, the memory of their hands, their feet, their eyes and their voices which, not so long ago, had goaded him to repeat precisely the patterns of his youth in the latter days of his life so that he might kiss those lips and clutch those hands once more, and search the whole world over, to put a girdle about the earth, if need be, seventy-seven times or more in search of his former darlings and their former embraces – all these had vanished.

Vanished: though the train still carried him twenty-four hours a day back to those old side streets, where, once upon a time on a spring morning he saw a young woman in a window, leaning on the ledge in her white night-gown, her hair still a little wild, her eyes still sleepy, one cheek still red from resting on the pillow, and Sindbad made friendly conversation with her before impulsively slipping in to join her, this strange woman in an unknown town. The adventure ended happily enough and twenty years later, on his next visit to the town, he saw a dark-haired young man in the window, learning his lessons. 'He could well be a younger version of me,' thought Sindbad.

But now, this early autumn day, they were all gone from his mind, and only the serious, firm-minded Monkey remained, she who had never wanted anything from him but to love him steadfastly, from a distance.

Ages ago, Monkey lived in a lonely house in the outer suburbs of Buda, near the excise post where the tram ran as fast as the express, clattering and humming through the night, so that a sleepless man might occupy himself listening to it.

The janitor put down the boots he was mending, licked his fingers copiously, leafed through the registration book, found his glasses and concluded that Monkey had moved to another district.

'How could she bear to leave these ancient sumach trees* behind?' asked Sindbad.

'Dunno,' answered the janitor and slammed the book shut.

The sumachs were whispering in the autumn breeze, 'Heavens, it's Mr Sindbad', for there were nights when they had sighed to him.

The janitor picked up the boots and pushed his glasses up on to his forehead. 'Heavens, it's Mr Sindbad!' he cried, for there were nights when he had brought wine or beer from the nearby coffee-house for him when Monkey still lived there.

'What happened?' asked Sindbad.

'It was like this. One day she gave me her cat. She said she was bored of it. Then she threw her old preserving jars on the rubbish heap. She threw away her old velvet hat too. The hat bored her. She was bored with everything here. So she moved away.'

The janitor pinned a price on the boots he had mended. The boots crackled. 'I haven't opened the doors at night for anyone since Mr Sindbad stopped visiting.'

Sindbad strolled, preoccupied, from the distant single-storey house, where the well stood in the middle of the courtyard surrounded by sweet-scented sumach trees. He poked a few fallen autumn twigs with his stick.

'Could Monkey have changed?' he asked himself.

And he set off to follow the footprints of Monkey's black low-heeled shoes.

Monkey – sought by Sindbad throughout the length and breadth of Buda and Pest – sat in the window in her pink night-gown, leaning on the ledge and reading a novel by Paul de Kock, just as she had been twenty years ago. Seeing Sindbad trundling down Cat Street, she formed a trumpet with her hands and like a cheerful cabby bellowed from the fourth floor, 'Here, boy!'

Sindbad immediately recognised Monkey's voice, for in the whole of Hungary there was only one woman with a voice like that – half hunting horn, half child's rattle. He looked up and waited for Monkey to give him a graceful wave. The coast was clear. He ran up three steps at a time, arriving exhausted and breathless on the fourth floor.

Monkey was standing in the doorway of the hall, a little cigarillo in her mouth as usual. 'You had better go easy on those old pins,' she said, indicating Sindbad's legs. 'What the devil were you doing in Cat Street?'

'Looking for your ladyship!' answered Sindbad, throwing himself into a chair in the hall.

Monkey refused to believe him as usual. 'Some little floozie of yours lives down this way, I bet. I'll find out, you know, and give her a poke in the ribs. I don't like being cheated right before my eyes, Sindbad.'

Sindbad raised his hand as if taking an oath. 'It's you I'm looking for, Monkey. It's such a long time since I saw you. Last night or the night before I dreamt of you and have been looking for you since. You haven't forgotten me, have you?'

Monkey took the cigar from her mouth. 'No, my dear,' she answered a little downcast. 'It's not my way to forget people so quickly. Even though it's been three whole years since I even saw you, and now I am reading Paul de Kock once again. My only sins are the imaginary ones in my book. But come in, let me get a closer look at you.'

She led Sindbad from the dark hall into the room overlooking the street. There was the old furniture and the portrait of her ancient father who long ago had become merely an all-seeing image; there was the portrait of the dead child to whom Monkey had at one time been an aunt; and there was the sampler framed behind glass as a memorial to the same dead little girl. There was the silent old canary in the window. And there, thrown untidily on the armchair, was the same knitted scarf that had lain on it last time Sindbad came to visit her at her previous address. The woman raised Sindbad's chin to the light of the window and closely examined his face and his eyes, gently stroking his hair.

'You know, Sindbad,' she said after a short silence, 'sometimes I love you so much, I feel less like your lover – your discarded, abandoned and forgotten lover – than like your mother. I know you so well. It is as if I had given birth to you.'

Sindbad sat down in the armchair and waited while Monkey carefully turned down the page in her book, and put it back in the cupboard.

'It was you who bought me these Paul de Kock novels, remember? You wanted me to read them at home, alone. I have read nothing else since then.'

Sindbad hummed a little tune as he watched her: she hadn't changed in ten years. She was a healthy, strong, dark-blonde woman, between thirty and forty years of age, who went early to bed, rose early, and hadn't worn make-up for a very long time. She liked wearing slippers and cooking tasty meals. In her late teens she used to like riding in carriages with amusing men for company, enjoyed champagne to the sound of gypsy bands and flinging her silk skirt about when dancing. But she got bored with such things because, as she said, there were so many flighty and downright wicked women in Pest that she was ashamed to be seen with them. Wearing slippers was preferable.

'I thought you'd never leave those sumach trees in the Buda house,' Sindbad said, gently. 'I can't think why you moved back into Cat Street – which you left in disgust in your youth to move to quiet Buda. As far as I know this remains the area where dancers, singers and cabaret performers live. You haven't gone back to your old profession, have you, Monkey?'

'No, my dear,' answered the woman solemnly. 'I have my fine dresses, my expensive hats, but I only put them on when we go out together. For ten years you have been promising to take me to the circus. And for ten years I have not visited the circus, though I have never been so poor as to dispose of my finest dress and my best hat ...'

Sindbad knew from previous experience where such conversations tended to lead, so he quickly interrupted her. 'No accusations now, Monkey. You visited the circus often enough in your youth. The circus is very much like the music hall. There are clowns in both. And loud women.'

'But the horses ...'

'Horses, horses! I've seen enough of horses to last me the rest of my life. I really don't understand how a serious, retiring, decent woman like you can spend day and night thinking about circuses.'

'But Sindbad,' she argued, her face solemn, 'it's been ten years since you promised me the circus. Your back was aching and you couldn't sleep unless I stroked it. You said that when you got better you would take me to the circus and you've not done it. I go nowhere by myself nowadays, my dear. There isn't anybody else. Only you.'

Sindbad leant forward and stroked Monkey's hand. 'We've had enough fun in our lives, you and I, Monkey.

You yourself once danced in the chorus line ... Let me suggest something else. When spring comes, let's wait for a fine sunny afternoon, pack a picnic, and wander the Buda hills. We'll take a horse-drawn coach across the Danube and the bridge will echo to the horses drumming. The coachman will sound his horn and there will be a provincial couple sitting opposite us, continually asking if it's far to the Kaiser Baths.* The horses will canter on and the coach will roll cheerfully along the rails. There will be children kicking a ball in Széna Square and someone playing an accordion in one of those old wattle and daub inns. But we won't alight there, no, we'll keep going and the coachman will give his horn another toot and the provincial couple will ask about the Kaiser Baths again. The fragrance of the Buda hills will already be filling the coach, and we will sit beside each other like a happily married couple. I will be a retired civil servant and you my wife of twenty years. We'll have a respectable amount of money in the Serbian Bank in Buda, and will have long had our eyes on a house in St Lorincz, a place with a small garden where you can keep ducks and hens ...'

'You rascal!' cried Monkey, laughing and crying at the same time, and happily throwing her arms about Sindbad's neck.

'Well, isn't that a lot better than going to the circus?' asked a satisfied Sindbad.

'A hundred times better,' answered Monkey and her eyes shone as bright as a child's at Christmas. 'So it's off to the hills in the spring and we'll lie in the grass.'

'Yes, Monkey. And now tell me, what have you been doing since I last saw you?'

She shrugged her shoulders. 'Nothing. That's what I'm used to doing … Do you remember my dark handsome brother who sang ballads so beautifully at the music hall and worked for the railways? Do you remember him? The poor boy got into trouble of some sort and went to America, but no one knew because I baled him out. But, it cost me all I had.'

'The bonds too?'

'I just kept them in the cupboard and never used them.'

'Your jewels?'

'Heavens! since when have I cared tuppence for jewellery? That's all in my foolish past.'

Sindbad shook his head and pondered. 'A pity your brother had to sing so much,' he grumbled.

'It's all the same now. I moved back into Cat Street, back into the house where I once owned the entire first floor and where Mitrovics the driver hung about the street all day waiting for me. And lords and earls would come and I would gad about with them, because I was young then. I'm back because I still have acquaintances here. Dancers from the clubs drop in for lunch with me. And I make a modest living out of that. If some little lordling should turn up now, I would kick him down the stairs.'

Sindbad quietly blew out smoke. 'Yes,' he muttered, 'you've always liked cooking.'

*

How did the story go?

Once Sindbad was dining with Monkey. There were six people around the table, with only one other man beside Sindbad in the company – the old gentleman in a skull cap and neatly arranged necktie who watched from the wall and hadn't opened his mouth in years. He was, after all, stuck in his gilded frame.

The ladies around the table, who all lived in the house in Cat Street, were, for the most part, wearing long housecoats. They had pulled these housecoats on over their underclothes, for they were not in the habit of dressing till the evening, when the big drum sounded and the band signalled the beginning of the next per-formance. Their hair, which would be beautifully coif-feured by clever hairdressers by the time evening came, was now brushed any old how, cascading over their foreheads and into their eyes. At first they regarded Sindbad with a certain interest, and the odd one even stuck her elegant and finely shod dancer's leg out from beneath her housecoat, but when it became apparent (over soup this was – a chicken soup with vegetables, just as Sindbad liked it) not only that Sindbad was unavailable, but that he was eating his soup under Monkey's jealous eye, the dancers took no more notice of him and consumed the rest of their dinner without recourse to cutlery. All artistes, in the privacy of these four walls they smacked their lips, licked their fingers and thoroughly enjoyed their food, as if knives and forks, like girdles and mascara, were merely reminders of their sad lives, their gay and melancholy profession. It was day now, noon, and the evening lay in the distant future; they took great pleasure in their eating. One of them, a soft-featured, reddish-haired woman, started to sing a peasant ditty she had heard back in the village. It was a song sung by army recruits: 'If only my mother could see me in the city ...' The women listened attentively to her passionate rendering, one or two with tears in their eyes. Who knows what they were thinking?

There was only one of them, a small-boned, flirtatious-eyed girl with a strange smile, who wouldn't let Sindbad alone. She kept rubbing her foot against his leg under the table, and on one occasion whispered to him, 'Come down to the music hall tonight.'

Monkey spotted this immediately, of course, and hissed at her, 'You snake. You serpent. Careful I don't poison you.'

The girl ran off, and not long after the others gathered themselves together, having toyed with the breadcrumbs and rolled them into little balls with their delicate fingers. Yawning and sleepy-eyed, hands in pockets, they dispersed to various corners of the house in Cat Street only to emerge in the evening – when the big drum thuds at the heart of the band – in great feathered hats and expensive dresses, decked out in jewels. There was to be no more eating with fingers, nor singing to their heart's content. They were on company time now. It was only at Monkey's dinners they could relax and be themselves.

'I see these trollops still hold a peculiar charm for you!' Monkey started up once she was alone with Sindbad. 'This lunch was intended as a test. I was curious whether you would retain your sang-froid, your composure, your indifference, in the company of four or five women, for so you ought by now, you ancient old roué. You were practically beside yourself with joy when that nasty piece of work started prodding your leg. Well, my dear, I told her where to get off. Because, as I said, this lunch was a test. I'm a poor unfortunate woman. You'll never change.'

Sindbad shrugged his shoulders. 'I don't understand your ladyship,' he grumbled. 'You bring on the dancing girls then complain when I'm not rude to them.'

Monkey's face was red with anger. 'You have to be rude to women like that! My God, if men knew women as I know them there'd be no more of this ridiculous talk of love. Understand, dear, that woman is creation's *coup de grâce*. And the young are the worst. Mind you, I wouldn't trust any of them, not even the old ones. A woman's mind is always set on destruction and she weaves her snares of love expressly for the destruction of men. She trades in jewels or in virtue. You want the spirit of the age? Think of an old frump. And no, dear, I will not tolerate a man in my rooms. Women have to behave decently here. Oh, they have offered me handsome amounts to allow them to entertain their rich gentlemen at home. But I have grown to despise money. I don't want much: honour, order, decency. *Honour!* There's something worth having in a life. And you know, that may be precisely why my dancers come to me. Not that it is easy to get a room here. Not everyone enjoys the favour of my lunches. Those who have been my lodgers speak well of me. Here, the sick are cured, the thin grow fat, and I don't allow them to throw their money away. They come to me in rags and in disgrace, and they leave wealthier and better dressed. Because I'm honest. I trade neither in jewels nor in virtue.'

Sindbad listened to Monkey, nodding the while. Yes, in many ways he too held her conduct in high respect. And he wasn't slow to tell her this.

Monkey accepted the praise but the flush of anger still burned on her cheek. She threw some seeds to the silent old canary then smoothed her dress and sat down opposite Sindbad again. 'In the past, when I first had the good fortune of your acquaintance, I didn't want to upset you. Today, however, I can tell you straight – now that we're on the subject – that I know every woman you've been in love with these last ten years ...'

'It was always only you,' answered Sindbad.

'For all I know you may be thinking of someone else this very moment. Because I *know* you, as well as if I had given birth to you. I knew when you loved me and when you didn't love me. My own love has not changed a jot. It's strange, I know, I hardly understand myself. I fell in love with you ten years ago and immediately I knew I would love you for the rest of my life. Even if you had died, Sindbad, I would not have forgotten you. Since I had the bad luck to fall in love with you – and sometimes I didn't see you for years – it was important for me to know what you were doing. That's why I enquired into your every step, learned about your affairs, investigated each of your loves. You never saw me, but you were never out of my sight. Even when you were asleep I was watching your sleeping face so I would know your dreams. I wanted to understand you, for I knew I couldn't live without you.'

'You went and bribed the servants,' observed Sindbad sharply.

'It's nothing to do with you how I knew about your affairs. Listen to this! You'll soon see I know everything.'

Monkey stepped over to the cupboard and took out a slim volume much like a prayerbook. 'This is where I used to write those things I didn't want to forget. Here we are. 21st June 19—. The lawyer K's wife lives apart from her husband and is waiting at the suspension bridge. 5 p.m. Sindbad arrives in closed car, number 37, the woman gets in. They spend two hours riding up and down behind drawn curtains in the Hidegkúti Road. This ride is repeated every week from June to October. During the same period the lawyer K's wife leaves her husband every Wednesday afternoon and strolls arm in arm with a blond officer on Fisherman's Bastion.* Two mornings a week she spends her time at the salon of the well-known couturier, Madame X, which several prominent men are known to frequent.'

Sindbad jumped to his feet. 'That's a lie. She was an honourable woman.'

Monkey flicked her hand as if waving away a fly. 'I'm not in the habit of lying, my dear. I know what I know. You were head over heels in love with that woman. True, I felt quite sorry for you then, but I didn't want your disillusion to come as too much of a shock. I allowed time to do its work. And lo and behold, here you are beside me again and it seems you love me. Let's move on. May, 19—. Flora M. is a secretary in the director X's office. A little round thing, brown-haired with a slight squint. Sindbad escorts her home every night for weeks and months on end till he succeeds in seducing her, then immediately leaves her. The seduction takes months because Flora M. is desperately in love with one of the firm's representatives to whom she eventually becomes engaged ...'

'You're a devil, Monkey. I've always thought of that woman as a beautiful but sad dream, the kind one sometimes awakes from to a tear-soaked pillow.'

Monkey continued in stiff formal tones. 'The representative was replaced by another. And that's the sum total of Flora's existence.'

One night – it was autumn going on winter and the snow was falling softly outside – Sindbad woke from his sleep with a sharp pain in his heart. Images from his dream still flickered before him; it was the usual dream of that time, women's faces, some in hats, some bare-headed, painted and unpainted faces; women's eyes, girls' eyes, all fixed on him in the same way as though Sindbad were the only man in the world; images of bare shoulders and stockinged legs with high-heeled shoes; then a long line of women in slips, women known to Sindbad, women he'd like to have known; plump arms, slender arms, every one of which was clasped about his neck, a generation of womankind trembling under the covers, performing somersaults in the pastures of his heart ...

He woke and the procession of dream women faded in the half-light like a lantern carried by some housewife across a snow-covered yard on a winter evening. For a while the glow of the lamp may be seen against a wall or haystack; a dark-haired female figure sways on the ripples of darkness, then the last woman, bright-eyed, wearing a feathered hat, finally disappears in the far distance – leaving Sindbad alone with his heartache. And shortly after this he began to feel ever more certain that very soon, perhaps within the hour, he would die.

He dressed quickly and sat down on the divan. At first he was very frightened because he had secretly believed that somehow he could put the whole thing off, despite the fact that he had been seriously ill recently and his voice sounded husky and strange, like the voice of a childhood friend overheard in the next room. Perhaps that lad, Bignio … whenever he found himself engaged in absent-minded desultory conversation it was the voice of young Bignio he heard talking somewhere in the neighbouring room.

'I shall shortly be dead,' he said to himself, breaking the sentence into distinct syllables. 'Yes, yes. I can hear young Bignio talking in the next room again.'

Of course, it was only in the first moments of his fear that Sindbad spoke aloud in the empty room, because, somehow, eventually, he recovered his composure: he could move his paralysed eyelids once more, and the pain relaxed its grip on his heart.

He stood up and stepped out onto the balcony where a thin layer of snow-covered tubs of flowers left over from the summer. It was dawn, the town was asleep and invisible snowflakes drifted around his head in cold draughts. He stared out into the hushed darkness for a

while without thinking – then suddenly he saw himself
in short child's boots and a little fur coat, ambling down
a path beside an old church, over weeds that had been
trodden into the snow. There were rooks sitting on the
cross surmounting the spire, and a red-cheeked brightly
dressed woman was approaching, carrying a bucket of
water from the icy well nearby. The dream town lay all
about him and he marched along down the weed- and
snow-covered path … Having passed the church he
noticed other things: at a window with white curtains, a
portly and mature woman turned her enormous eyes on
him, her nose crooked, a grotesquely sensuous smile on
her lips, a smile he might have seen somewhere before,
if only for a moment a long time ago … then the image
was gone and he was simply standing on the balcony
again while endless flurries of snow swept by him.

And as he stepped from the balcony back into the
room, it was still the hook-nosed older woman of his
childhood he was thinking of, the woman he had seen
so long ago and had practically forgotten. Now he saw
her again and felt her fat white arms, her swollen
shoulders and her brown back creased with fat. There
was a mole there somewhere too … her fingers had
shiny little white nails, and those white nails were
touching the young Sindbad in a spellbindingly feminine way. He feels those dazzling feminine nails first on
his feet, then on his brow, then across his chest. The
wide lips twist into that grotesque smile and he hears a
sound, part sigh, part hiss, above his head. It's as if a
bird had flown across the room.

Sindbad's Dream

Once again Sindbad felt bands tightening about his heart, so he decided he would make final preparations for his impending death. He wrote a few lines to Monkey informing her of his condition. 'I'll be gone by the morning.' The servant at the inn took his note and meandered down the stairs, whistling merrily in anticipation of a handsome tip. Perhaps he thought number 5 was sending him on another errand of love, much as he used to in the past, when his task was to bring nightly supplies of champagne, tea, cigarettes and stuff from the pharmacy and there was plenty of silver for him to slip into his waistcoat pocket.

While he was about his business Sindbad lay down on the worn old rug, because that was what he felt like doing. He spread his arms out and stared rigidly and desperately at the lamp above him. As long as he could see its two bulbs he was all right. So he kept looking at the two bulbs which used to shine with such peculiar brightness when they cast their light across the shoulders of a long succession of women.

Until now he had always felt a great sense of calm looking at the light, but now one of the bulbs gave a sudden wheeze. Immediately the other one groaned. It sounded like a chronic invalid turning on his bed ... Somewhere, some time in the past, his father, his beautiful melancholy father, was lying on the bed. It was New Year's Eve and the young Sindbad was holding his hands.

'You'll make the new year, father. The new year will bring good luck.'

The invalid opened his sad and hopeless eyes. 'You think so?' he asked and shook his head.

Sindbad suddenly wished him a quick death, so that his father should not have to suffer any more. There'd be no more groans and cries of pain …

'My estate, doctor. If only I could live another week …'

Yes, those were the words. He had died prematurely. Now Sindbad seemed to hear one light bulb repeat those words to the other.

One more woman's body, or simply part of her body, flashed before him: full, white, a globe of alabaster. And he could see the blue-black shadow creep across that globe, and was aware of a variety of delicious, well-remembered perfumes wafting about his head.

Soon Monkey arrived and tenderly closed Sindbad's eyes for him.

Sindbad became a sprig of mistletoe. A sprig of mistletoe in the rose garland an elderly nun wore about her waist. For a while, he had a rather boring time of it. He regretted he had not chosen some other occupation when he had had the opportunity to do so at the bureau where men are allotted tasks in their life after death. Having run his eye down all the posts available there were three he particularly fancied, where he thought he might be able to spend his days in silence and idleness. One was as a toy soldier, better still a toy soldier lost in some dim attic. What more could a man longing for retirement want? Sindbad had all but signed up to this when a grey-bearded goldsmith appeared at the bureau with an agonised expression on his face and a gaping hole in his temple where the bullet had entered. He had killed himself on account of certain women, for whose sake he had given away the contents of his shop. Sindbad's heart was moved at the sight of the woeful-looking little man; he thought of the men whom women had cheated, stolen from and discarded, men whom women had watched with interest, wondering when they would put a bullet through their brains – so he gave up the idea of being a soldier allowing the goldsmith to take precedence in the choice.

In considering his subsequent career he was equally tempted by the thought of becoming an ornamental comb. But how was one to know where one would wind up? The woman might be dirty. Sindbad had decided he might as well stay alive, and this is how he became a sprig of mistletoe in a rose garland. Not too many risks there: it was hard to get into scrapes in such a situation, he would still feel the touch of women's hands and some people enjoy this long after they are dead. Unfortunately the nun into whose possession he came, who wore him about her waist, was a little too old for him: she ground him between her fingers as she muttered her prayers but these, alas, were of little interest to him. It was a fairly dull set of pleas and prayers that pulsed through his body. There was a prayer for sound digestion, one for deep sleep, another for protection from the severity of the Mother Superior, and only once something that referred, somewhat obscurely, to a certain Brother Francis. Sindbad pricked up his ears. It couldn't be, could it? thought the sprig. No, unfortunately the Francis

referred to was just a saintly old man who had caught a
bad chill at midnight mass and was lying on his sickbed
in the rectory. Sindbad grew very bored of this constant
diet of virtue and sanctity and reflected painfully on the
fact that he was not made for a high moral existence and,
if things went on like this, he'd never reach the happy
state of having purged his sins. He began to regret ever
more intensely that he hadn't chosen to be a toy soldier.
Who knows what adventures he might have had? But
he'd just as happily have been an ornamental comb on
the head of a whore: it was the present state of grace he
couldn't tolerate.

One day the nun and the sprig went on a journey. They
rattled through the convent gates in a wide leather-
topped carriage drawn by stout horses, and consequently transferred to a train – travelling in the
women's compartment, of course – where the nun made
the acquaintance of two elderly ladies who were full of
stories of railway disasters. The conversation only became interesting when one of the old women happened
to mention that she couldn't be a nun because she
couldn't live without men … 'My old man is a real
gem,' said she, blushing but proud. The nun cast her
eyes down but later asked the woman her husband's age,
enquiring about his looks and habits and so on. Of her
answers Sindbad noted only those relating to her
husband's habits: once he'd had a glass or two he would
even go up to the attic for her and fetch the clothes she
had hung out to dry there the previous week.

Before the other old lady could interject an account
of the heroic deeds of her late husband the train reached

the station, they got off, and Sindbad suddenly became aware that he was no longer attached to the pious nun's skirts which he, being a sprig of mistletoe, had practically worn through by continuous friction. A happy accident had separated them. Sindbad had fallen between the rails: trains passed over him, firemen threw fiery ashes over him and a piece of greaseproof paper landed in his vicinity, containing the remnants of a well-chewed leg of duck. This unpleasant neighbour attempted to strike up some kind of relationship with him but Sindbad pretended to be asleep until night came, then succeeded in escaping without being observed, leaving the rails behind and drifting into the town which he immediately recognised.

Good heavens! Wasn't this the town he had visited just before his death? Why didn't he notice the tunnel they passed through just before the station? It was a small mountain town full of cheerful gold miners. During the day the entire population spent its time searching for gold in the valleys while dwarfs left their windows open for ventilation, revealing their hoards of hidden gold. Here was the mayor, the priest, the school teacher. But once night fell the town was lit up and everyone was having a good time. We shall never die, they say to themselves, there's enough gold in those mountains. There was singing of songs, playing of instruments, the clinking of glasses and the sound of women laughing as though someone were tickling them. Sindbad had an acquaintance here who married a gold miner. The story of this acquaintance, a certain Paula, originated from the time the gold miner came up to Pest and asked her parents for her hand in marriage. Paula kissed Sindbad when no one was looking and whispered into his ear that when she was an old woman and bored with her husband, and if he still considered her attractive, he could find her and visit her. That's how Sindbad found himself in the mining town: and the miner's wife showed him her jewels, her expensive fur and her coach and four. I beg your pardon, said Sindbad. I have come too early. He left, and with a chalk drew a cross on the gate so he should not forget the house when he came that way again. But in the meantime he died … and became a sprig of mistletoe. Nevertheless he soon found the gate and shortly afterwards was to be found in her room.

The gold miner's wife sat in front of the mirror, combing her hair. She had long golden hair and the comb ran lightly through it like a boat gliding across the water. Up and down moved the comb – at that moment it was the proudest utensil in the whole house, not surprisingly, since in its previous life it had been a mere dancing master in one of the outer suburbs of Pest. 'I too could have been a comb,' thought Sindbad, but tried to remain unobserved.

The comb glowed brighter and brighter with pride, to the great envy of the mirrored wardrobe and the silk-covered bed. The bed linen was of silk such as you find only in the beds of kings and gold miners. Delicious perfumes mingled together in her bedroom. Sindbad stretched out – in so far as a sprig of mistletoe can stretch – and thought what an ass he was not to have escaped from his former mistress earlier.

After combing her hair the woman took off all her clothes. She was like a dream of snow. She moved about the room, stroked a silk skirt that was thrown across the back of a chair, gave a sigh, then disappeared into the silken bed. Then she turned off the light.

By the Danube

indbad once spent a melancholy time in a small village by the Danube, trying to heal his sick mind and troubled heart. He was staying with strangers and there was only a shadowy veranda where he could stretch his legs out. (He practically had to get down on all fours in order to enter the peasant cabin.) This was where he lived, forgotten by everyone, watching from the veranda as the great Danube, wide as a lake at this particular stretch, flowed by in front of him. In the evening a lamp burned on the opposite bank sending rays of light across the black water. During the day sooty tugs made their way downriver, stopping now and then to drop anchor, their little red and white pennants seeming to wave directly at Sindbad as if the boats had hesitated by the village expressly to greet him. (On these occasions Sindbad would imagine a taciturn walrus-moustached steersman, puffing his pipe somewhere in the stern of the noisy tug while his wife washed his shirt in the lifeboat.) In the afternoon the pot-bellied Vienna packet sliced through the waves, floundering on, grace-less as a fat priest. Its paddles solemnly shoved water aside and the deck above was set with white-covered tables off which portly foreigners ate cold ham and sipped at chilled beer while women and girls in brightly coloured dresses leaned on the rails wearing wide straw hats and waved their handkerchiefs at Sindbad. (At such times Sindbad would have liked to have been a ship's officer in white trousers and gold braided cap. He would be wearing white shoes and dreamily pacing the deck, casting winning glances at the large-eyed Romanian women in their raw silk gowns.) Then the Vienna packet disappeared round the bend and Sindbad was left with the distant ruins on the hills opposite. Once there were kings living among those hills and the trees had not quite obscured the road along which the kings drove to the castle, wearing velvet cloaks and great clinking spurs, their ladies beside them. The ladies' dresses had high waists and gold-embroidered satin skirts. They wore boots, since they frequently went riding and would gallop along the flat shore with curly-headed youths in their wake. Though the Danube washed the very foot of the hills the women tended not to bathe there as it was not fashionable at the time. (Sindbad also wanted to be a friar confessor in the castle chapel, and hear the ladies' confessions while blindfolded with a white scarf. He was sure that confessions could be trusted in those days – not like now. Hell, after all, was far closer then. The friar had only to mutter the word and the devil himself would appear at the door. Sindbad particularly wanted to grant absolution to the wife of King Louis the Great, at the castle chapel, preferably during Passion Week ...)

Then evening fell. Hills, forests, castles and red-roofed peasant houses faded in the descending gloom, but a rowing boat glimmered faintly on the silvery

Danube, and in that boat sat a number of women in white, their white veils fluttering above the water. Then the jetty lamplighter appeared in the darkness on the far shore and silence settled on the great river. Silent and unseen the ripples ran on carrying news of Sindbad to distant seas, telling of his melancholy as he sat on the rickety veranda in the small village. (If those ripples travel far enough, thought Sindbad, they should arrive at a remote province of some foreign country where a buxom dark-eyed oriental woman is certain to be washing her round white knees in the waves of the Danube. And those cool ripples will suddenly give way to a warm current which will embrace those white legs. These would be the waves on which Sindbad's eyes had lingered so desirously, there between the tall hills.) Then it was night, and at last Sindbad's friends, the trains, appeared and rushed along the high embankments.

The veranda from which Sindbad looked out in his seclusion, offered a fine view of the embankment which ran plumb through the middle of the village, the embankment down which one hundred and fifty carriages thundered each and every day. In the daytime the engines provided entertainment for Sindbad: the huge black contraptions rolling along at an enormous rate presented themselves in his imagination as living beings. They were great, proud irritable creatures who only visited the region because they had to. The monstrous American-style express trains blasted the small village with one or two puffs of smoke before disappearing. The little top hats raced beyond the tops of the trees, the big wheels turned so fast you'd have thought it was their last day on earth and the iron bridge gave a respectful shudder as if greeting a well-known but highly respected visitor for whom it was unnecessary to lay on a more ceremonious welcome. 'Eee-egh,' muttered the iron bridge and the Buffalo engine was already flying beyond the town, so that within a few minutes only the hills still echoed its rapid panting. Lanky telegraph poles stared frightened, almost bewildered, at the row of carriages with well-bred ladies and gentlemen at the windows, at the white tablecloths and wine flasks flashing by inside the dining car where the cook in his chef's hat gazed out, and at the sooty contemplative fireman frowning on the footplate. The long carriages hurried towards their destination and in the gangway of the very last one a man and a woman were holding hands. (Naturally, Sindbad imagined himself on his honeymoon, seated on a green davenport, gazing intently into the eyes of some young girl, as if for the first time, while the white-coated porter interrupted them with a knock at the door to inform them that dinner was being served ...)

By now the train sounds no more than a distant coughing and the rattling is a long way off. The wide funnel hoves briefly into sight as it rounds a bend, and thick black smoke is pouring out and settling on the landscape. Ho-ho-ho ... cries the engine as it rolls across the iron bridge and the engine driver in his blue jerkin and his sooty hat is absorbed in the prospect of the rails before him as he leans out of the window. The white steam hisses and darts past the wheels, and the engine flue is like a tax office clerk's hat when he goes to pay his respects to his boss on the first day of the year. The faded and dusty passenger cars follow each other with apparent indifference but in the train, behind the windows, life in all its variety is in progress: round-eyed children gawp at the village; plump mothers have removed their stays and sprawl comfortably on the leather seats, nibbling at ham bones spread out on serviettes; men in shirt-sleeves laugh loudly, joking with the women; and one bald man is carefully drawing the curtains closed while strains of cheerful singing emanate from the end of the train. A choir of young peasant girls in the third-class carriage join in a tune, young lads wave their hats in the middle of the compartment. The conductors are bright-eyed young men with fine twisted moustaches bellowing out the name of each station, saluting military fashion to a plump widow in a black dress and white stockings, who slowly descends the steep steps wearing a complacent smile. The girls with the wind-tousled hair – they might be teachers or governesses with newly earned diplomas making their way to some distant town – sport white blouses, and lean out of the departing train's window, their arms exposed, casting a few flirtatious glances at the figure of Sindbad loitering on the platform. A perspiring man in linen trousers leans across the soft-shouldered girls and a tall thin girl pinches his arm. The train draws away, a cheeky young peasant bride in the third class pulls her skirts up at Sindbad by way of greeting and the conductors swagger broad-chested on the steps. (Now Sindbad rather fancied being a railway conductor: he imagined stepping white-gloved into the ladies' compartment where a blushing bride was sitting in *déshabillé* because of the heat, asking him complicated questions about the timetable, and having answered them the conductor would quietly close the door behind him.)

And at night, when the express rushes almost silently across the high embankment, the engine seems to be flying on its well-oiled wheels, the lamps cast long beams of light along the rails and the carriages roll steadily along. When behind open windows striking women of foreign appearance are taking their clothes off in the sleeping compartments and men wearing military decorations are reading broadsheets in the dining car, and you pick up that blend of Havana and cologne even through the smell of coaldust, then Sindbad becomes a sleeping car attendant with a black moustache and a Henry VIII beard, in a gold braided hat, who calmly and elegantly steps into the sleeping compartments, approaches the lovely Romanian woman who is already dozing and asks, in a cool but delicate manner, 'Is there anything else I could get you, madam?' And the express rolls steadily down the rails while people dowse their candles in the little peasant houses rapidly disappearing behind them, and husband and wife quietly lie down together.

Somewhere, far off in the night, the faint lights of a melancholy freight train are blinking and the driver is sitting in his cabin, his cap drawn over his eyes, drawing deeply on his pipe.

No, Sindbad did not spend very much time thinking of that freight train the summer he spent by the Danube.

Sindbad and the Actress

It happened once that Sindbad was travelling by coach ... It was late at night and the full moon was hiding behind raincoat-shaped clouds. Sindbad sat silently in the middle of the carriage gazing at the driver's shoulders. Occasionally the wind whistled across the fields: it was getting towards autumn and Sindbad wondered how he had become involved in this present adventure. Why should he be speeding down the highway at night, across marshy ground in a damp wind when he could be sleeping soundly in his own bed? How had this come about?

Sindbad – who was a youth of merely a hundred years then – was going to spend some time with a friend in the country. He had always liked those old country cottages where the walls were covered with images of his father's and grandfather's contemporaries. Sitting beside those ancient fireplaces he remembered tales told to him by his grandmother while his beautiful sad-eyed mother sat at a delicate sewing table stitching canvas in the blush of twilight. It was as if the very servants were those who had busied themselves about him in his childhood. Isn't that uncle János, the liveried old village clerk? Pity his name is actually Miska. Surely he must be some late descendant of uncle János: after all, these liveried clerks tend to succeed each other in dynasties.

The host is the jolly sort who likes a bit of entertainment, a certain Kápolnai by name. Goes riding in the morning, takes a turn around the estate, then sits down at noon to a hearty meal. And here's the village choirmaster from his youth. He sits at the end of the table and once he gets a few glasses of wine down him he waxes lyrical, treating the assembled company to a homily full of fine rhetorical flourishes. There's a stork's nest on the chimney stack and the guard dog is called Tisza, after the river* ... Sindbad would often sit down to consider how it was that an entire world, a world that was supposed to have disappeared some time ago, could so resurrect itself before him. It was as if Hungarian village life had remained unchanged over the centuries. The people had changed but they had been replaced by others precisely like them. As if birth, death and marriage were all part of some curious joke. Even now it was the ancestral dead sitting around the table. They reproduced themselves: women, children. The weathercock spins, the wind and rain beat on the roof precisely as before, and neither the cloud approaching from the west nor the meadow stretching far into the distance appears to realise that the man sitting at the window is of this century not the last. Snow falls, logs from the forest crackle in the fire. The current host is rubbing his hands before the stove just as his ancestor used to do. It's plain as plain could be that grandfather and great-grandfather, who stare down from the walls, are still very much here, and have never gone away. When spring comes round they'll stand behind the host and whisper in his ear: time to sow rape seed in the meadow ... and it will be done.

There was a woman in the house too. She was a quiet, pale young thing. But Sindbad knew very well that these white anaemic brides would sooner or later turn into ruddy-faced, round-bosomed countrywomen, for this was precisely what their grandmothers had become. And she would administer a sound box on the ear to the farmhand should occasion demand it. Then, grey-haired, she would dance at a grandchild's wedding, before finally taking up residence on the wall, rendered into oils and framed in gilt so as to observe succeeding women's fates, joys and sorrows.

So Sindbad the house-guest was not too concerned about the woman's pallor and sadness. She had no children yet, that was why she was always knitting babies' bonnets.

She was called Etelka, and she would disappear from the table without anyone noticing when the choir-master launched on one of his more ribald anecdotes. The choir-master, who was a solid drinking man, was invariably handed over to the servants at the end of the festivities and they would lead him home. On one such occasion the host leaned over to his guest and said: 'I'm putting Etelka to the test tomorrow. Tomorrow evening we shall go into town, to the theatre ...'

Sindbad puffed at his cigar, pondered a while, then asked quietly: 'Your wife wasn't an actress by any chance?'

Kápolnai shook his head. 'Not precisely, only in a manner of speaking. Her parents were foolish, ambitious folk and sent her to study acting. They thought she'd find a husband all the sooner if she were on the stage. But as it turned out, I met her at the May fair. I'd never seen her on stage.'

'Then what happened?'

'For a long time she kept turning me down because she was so attached to the theatre. I persisted of course. They led her on. They told her she had talent. That she would become a world-famous actress.'

'Nevertheless she married you?'

'Yes, because I promised her that should it happen that she no longer wanted to be my wife, that day she could go back on the stage again. I wouldn't prevent her.'

Sindbad drew deeply on his cigar. He glanced around the cottage which was just beginning to give itself up to the mild summer night. The wind crept silently under the vine leaves in the yard. 'I wouldn't advise you to put her to the test. Stay at home tomorrow.'

Kápolnai shrugged. 'Too late now. I've promised her.'

Next night Sindbad was so generous with the wine that the choir-master made his own way home. It was midnight and his hosts had still not returned. Sindbad sat preoccupied on the veranda. He knew the theatre in town was performing *Rip van Winkle* that night. In his boredom he recalled the whole operetta and all the actresses he had gaped at in the spotlight while clutching Lisbeth's tarlatan* skirt. Once more he saw the fine ankles and smiling eyes. From far away the melody of the chorus rose out of the night, and brushed past his ear like a moth: 'By cliff-verged paths – the trail leads on …' they sang.

He heard the noise of trap wheels approaching rapidly down the road: Kápolnai and his wife returning from the theatre.

His host was undoubtedly in a foul mood, but Etelka's face was glowing and her eyes were so bright Sindbad almost took a step backwards in surprise when she looked at him. She kissed her husband two or three times before retiring to her room.

'Thank you. Thank you,' she kept repeating in her gratitude.

Kápolnai bitterly drained a glass of wine. 'You were right,' he said, clearing his throat. 'The test came a little too soon. We've only been married two years.'

'Well, how did she take it?'

'In the strangest possible way. Once we were in the theatre she immediately discovered old acquaintances, actors and actresses sitting in the auditorium. First she gathered them in one of the boxes, then she went back-stage to meet the leading lady. A down-at-heel comedian, old before his time, reminded her what wonderful times they had had at drama school. The squinting pot-bellied manager, the liar, had the nerve to tell her that her old contract was still stored away in his desk. I ordered him to give it back at once. The rogue laughed at me and said, who knows, she might need it sometime. An actor! You know what that word means? It means everything that is low, frivolous and rotten. And she, my wife, felt happy there, in that company of actors.'

Sindbad hummed a few sympathetic noises and fairly soon bid the man goodnight. It was no surprise to him to see the two of them sitting and frowning at each other the next morning. That afternoon he heard the sounds of a furious row in progress.

A couple of days later he was walking in the fields for most of the day and returned late in the evening. He found Kápolnai on the veranda, his face in his hands. 'Etelka has left me to become an actress,' he said, in a low strangled voice.

This is how it came about that Sindbad was travelling by night in a hired coach (Etelka had gone off in the family trap), seeking the woman in an attempt to persuade her to return.

He tried to defend himself from the cold night wind by entertaining himself with all kinds of foolish thoughts. Among other things he considered the option of the love-lorn Kápolnai himself taking to the stage in competition with his wife, should she prove impervious to argument. He'd look good in patent leather boots and cockade. He could start in the chorus and watch his wife from there, eyes burning, while she flirted with the audience.

It was morning by the time they arrived at a tiny provincial town. The houses were still half asleep and uncombed women stood in doorways regaling each other with their dreams. The coach lumbered down a long street: the road was thick with mud but, under the mud, sly stones crept under the carriage wheels. It was as if the citizens had placed the stones there expressly for the reception of their country cousins. A school-teacherly figure was ambling towards the school, his arms folded, then a baker's apprentice went by with a piercing whistle, the whole street resounding to his call. The tower at the end of the long road seemed to be waking up, its head still enveloped in mist, vaguely blinking. Vegetables shone, green and fresh, in the gardens. Only the poplars stood bitter and unmoving on the pavement, indifferent to the world around them. They dropped a leaf or two into Sindbad's carriage as he passed.

The inn was called The Golden Elephant and it looked as dark and sombre as something from an old English novel. The innkeeper, a suspicious, bearded Jew, examined Sindbad from head to toe. Sindbad asked him about the missing woman.

'Is the gentleman a traveller?' asked the innkeeper.

'No.'

'I only ask,' the proprietor of The Golden Elephant warned him, 'because there would have been no point in telling me he was. He has no luggage. No luggage, no reduction in room tariff.'

Sindbad enquired again about the woman.

'No women of any kind in my place,' the innkeeper answered and led him upstairs by a dangerous rickety set of steps. The room was low-ceilinged and damp, and Sindbad looked at the bed with trepidation. On the wall he discovered a picture. It showed various members of the royal family. Communing silently with them, Sindbad eventually closed his tired eyes.

When he went out in the afternoon there was a brilliant scarlet poster nailed to the prison-like walls of The Golden Elephant. The company had arrived in town and would give a performance that night in the Elephant's banqueting hall. The worthy townspeople are hereby invited thereto by Dummy Dunai, director of the theatre.

'That's it!' cried Sindbad. 'Here's Etelka.'

He spent some time in the coffee-house watching the comings and goings, but eventually the constant smoking and spitting of the guests annoyed him and he left. He wandered about town, glancing at shop displays ancient enough to have tempted him in his childhood. He admired the likeness of the chief of the fire brigade in the photographer's window. Behind the mallow-coloured curtains of the café he noted a dark-haired, doe-eyed young woman with a faint moustache. She was wearing a white pinafore and arranging cream cakes on a tray. He ducked into the lemon-and-vanilla-scented shop and made strenuous efforts to get acquainted with the brown-haired girl who was at first rather frightened of such a complete stranger. Later she confessed her name was Irma ... but just as they got to this point Sindbad remembered the fugitive Mrs Kápolnai, quickly paid the bill and was gone, though he would happily have stayed in the café. He ambled aimlessly about town while country women and young girls giggled into their handkerchiefs at him then hastened on. An old officious-looking man examined Sindbad's patent leather boots with clear distaste. Then the ginger-moustached proprietor of the barber shop made a loud approving remark to his customers on the subject of Sindbad's neatly styled hair.

Eventually it was evening. Sindbad took his place in the front row and, not without a certain excitement, waited for the curtains to rise. Slowly the auditorium filled up …

And in the third act, to the accompaniment of a harsh-toned piano, Etelka stepped forward. Yes, yes: she wore a pink corset and the same shoes she had worn at home. Her face was highly rouged and a small sword hung by her side. She appeared from the wings, singing in a weak voice, her hands clasped to her heart. Sindbad saw her blank frightened look. A more sonorous voice rang out in the audience: 'Louder, young lady!'

Scuffling, murmuring, hushing: other voices immediately demand 'Silence!' The song halts in mid note and Etelka stands on the stage, terrified, tears filling her eyes. Both her hands are trembling.

Sindbad in the front row claps his hands together as loudly as he can. Others take up the applause and someone is shouting something at the back. The woman's eye falls on Sindbad. The blood drains from her face. She looks like a wounded deer. An actor in a wig hurries forward from the wings. He holds out his arms to Etelka and leading her away, cries to the audience, 'The young lady is unwell.'

The conductor hammers at the keys of the piano. The audience slowly falls quiet again, only to burst out laughing when the fat comic appears on stage, scuttling on all fours …

'What are you doing here?' the woman asks later, her voice unsteady. She has dressed and taken a few deep lungfuls of fresh air out in the yard.

'I came for you. Your husband sent me.'

'I'll go home if you promise never to tell anyone you saw me in a corset.'

Winter Journey

n the night hours, when Sindbad laid his head down
on the pillow and thoughts swirled about his head
like departing birds of passage, ever fewer in number
and ever further off; and later, in the morning, while the
warm kisses of the previous night's dream still lingered
with him in bed under the covers, on the soft cushion,
or lay tangled in the woolly weave of the carpet; when
the aristocratic woman in the black silk dress and scarlet
mask, the woman of his dreams, was still standing on
the threshold in her lacquered ankle boots and delicate
silk stockings, the kind court ladies wear without the
queen's knowledge – at such times, a dark-haired little
actress dressed in black with black silk stockings and
an eagle's feather in her hat would often come to visit
him in his lonely room, the hair behind her ears soft and
loose but freshly combed, just as Sindbad the sailor had
last seen her.

So often did the actress visit Sindbad in these half-
dreamt, half-experienced hours of pleasure that one day
he decided to seek her out.

He remembered adventures of years gone by, in the
melancholy days of his youth, when he had been subject
to mysterious dreams and fantasies in which two hearts

seemed to rise like swallows from a shared nest only to fly off in opposite directions.

A day came when he thought it possible that somehow, somewhere, this actress – whom he had already forgotten once – might herself, under her own bedclothes, be preoccupied with just such hidden and passionate thoughts of him as he of her when he imagined her sweet heart-shaped face a mere inch from his on the pillow.

It was possible that somewhere she desired him: her affections might be undirected or disengaged so she would have only memories to console her; that she was dreaming of the face of a man long gone because, as things were, there was not one neatly curling beard, nor one set of dashing moustaches reflected in the mirror of her heart.

After he had thought these things over a few times, Sindbad roused himself and set out in search of her, though his hair had turned as grey as the wings of the arctic tern that used to swoop over the clashing waves of the Danube. The trail that harsh winter led him to the town of Eperjes.*

Deep snow lay about the town like fortifications; old houses were tightly shut against blizzards as if fearing the approach of a besieging army. People protected their noses from the cold and Slovaks ambled down the street with long-haired ponies and carts of firewood. It was as if snowmen had come alive in some tale out of Hans Christian Andersen. It was only with difficulty that Sindbad found an innkeeper, a disreputable-looking man with intelligent eyes, who could tell him precisely which direction the group of travelling actors (Paula's company) took after leaving Eperjes. They were planning to cross the high hills on a rather fragile-looking train which clings to the hills' steep contours. But there were blizzards in the hills now: the little train might no longer be clinging to anything.

The actors were somewhere else, in Verhovina perhaps, or beyond by now, having left one royal cloak and a pair of courtly riding boots behind with the innkeeper as security.

Sindbad was rather glad he had not succeeded in finding Paula straightaway. She seemed rather more of a prize this way, an exotic finch taking refuge from approaching footsteps in the depths of the forest. 'I'll follow her!' he said to himself as he wandered down the street in the blizzard, looking in windows, enjoying the scent of unfamiliar women.

Then, near the stumpy snow-covered tower where the air was loud with cries of invisible rooks and jackdaws, he saw an elegant woman in a Russian style fur cap and a short fur jacket coming towards him down the cleared path. She wore smart shoes and a fashionable narrow skirt, but when she drew near he could see her face was tired and wasted. The once delicate nose was raw red from the cold and years of make-up; harsh narrow lines framed her listless mouth. Only the forget-me-not blue of her eyes still sparkled sweetness and youth at the passing Sindbad, who raised his hat. (Sindbad always greeted clergymen and well-bred ladies this way in the country, for he preferred them to think of him as a courteous man of religious temper, even if he remained unknown to them.)

The woman passed on and Sindbad turned round to look at her. He cast his eyes over her clothes, her shoes, her long elbow-length gloves again and thought she must be an ageing aristocratic maiden aunt. 'If Paula didn't exist I would follow her and stay in Eperjes!'

It was a gross misjudgment, as he realised later, sipping his after-dinner black coffee at the high chair of a coffee-house which turned out to be the domain of the said aristocratic lady. She was the wife of the owner. Once she had worked behind the counter in Pest, now she was carefully leafing through the illustrated magazines, her bracelets clinking about her solid wrist, and when she looked at him it was with a frosty superiority, in the manner of a married woman no longer interested in the conversation of strange men.

Later the gypsies appeared in queer light-coloured hard hats and cast-off dandy cloaks. The *primás*, or solo violinist, sported a painted moustache and kissed the lady's hand, asking if he might take the instruments piled in a corner to play at a wedding in the afternoon.

'Very well. But tell the band not to come back drunk, Zsiga,' she admonished him in a solemn, semi-maternal manner.

After they had gone Sindbad ordered a French cognac and, having attracted the stern woman's attention, soon succeeded in drawing a warm, almost complaisant smile from her. They looked hard at each other.

'No, it's impossible … quite impossible, at least not here …'

'But I find you very attractive. I am half in love with you already,' Sindbad answered with his eyes.

'Really?' asked the woman.

'Really,' Sindbad's almond-brown eyes assured her. 'But you mustn't be angry with me.'

The coffee woman fiddled with the sugar bowl. She raised her eyes. 'I am not angry,' answered her forget-me-not blue gaze. Later she adjusted her hair taking a secret peek in the mirror behind her.

It was time for the departure of the little train that clung to the steep hillside, so Sindbad left without taking another glance at her, regarding the flirtation as a job well done.

The night blizzard and the icy compartment, the impenetrable darkness outside, the screeching, squeaking and groaning of the wheels like so many apprentice ghosts, the rattling of the chains, the choked puffing of the engine and the warmth of his fur coat had a soporific effect on Sindbad. He consulted his watch. It was getting on for ten. Back in Eperjes the coffee-house owner would have donned his little black cap, and his wife would have lain down in her lonely bed. She would be pulling off her stockings, and the cinders in the iron stove would be glowing like animal eyes. Now she'd be tucking her plumpish body under the duvet, blowing out the candle, stretching herself for a second – or perhaps longer – and the strange gentleman who cast such amorous glances at her that afternoon in the coffee-house would cross her thoughts. Might he have left town?

From behind the low stove there appeared the cloaked knight whose care it was to watch over the dreams of women's rooms: silently he stepped forward, his ostrich-feathered cap perched on his head, and soon the woman's white arm was hugging the pillow as tenderly as if it had been Sindbad's neck.

The train was rumbling warily over the blasted and frozen plateau, fearing to disturb the dead lying beneath the snow-covered field. The wheels kept rolling. Whole hours might have gone by till eventually Sindbad gave a faint laugh and took leave of his first dream, the dream of the coffee-shop woman.

The train had stopped at a station. Beyond the carriage window snow was flying so fast one could be certain that somewhere, not too far off, wolves would be slinking along the highway towards the village in single file, their heads bent low. A lantern was being carried down the length of the platform in the dark, the voices of railworkers distant, faint, conspiratorial.

At last the chains rattled, the icy wheels screamed and the train trundled off again. As it left the midway station behind, Sindbad began to think of the slight figure of Paula with her dark hair. Where would he find her? And that dear little shoe of hers with the ribbon tied in a bow – what state would that be in now? Would the hair tucked behind her ears be clean and sweet-scented?

The winter afternoon, as if in recognition of the fact that these were red-letter days on the calendar, cast brilliant beams of pinky gold over the small border town under whose snow-covered roofs Sindbad was making his way past solidly frozen wooden bridges and niches from which carved stone saints peeked out, searching for the actress who went by the name of Paula. Yes, this is where the company of actors are staying and where night after night they gladden or sadden hearts at the Great Bercsényi inn.* Paula is the company's *ingénue,* heroine and mother figure all rolled into one, and at this precise moment she is learning her lines, pacing a sunlit garden at the edge of town, where once upon a time the castle chapel used to stand, the chapel past which resolute-looking noblemen and ladies with finely arched feet would stroll from the castle into town. Paula, who doesn't take lunch at the inn with the others, regards it as her favourite place – or so Sindbad was assured by the prompter, Pápai, an acquaintance of some three hundred years, for in his youth Sindbad frequently travelled to see performances in the country and would make a point of occupying the box nearest the stage. Pápai coughed, lisped and blew his nose into a large spotted handkerchief, then stuck a half-cigar between his teeth and tried vainly to strike a match against an old matchbox, but said nothing more of Paula.

Only at the end of the conversation did he append a comment of his own. 'Really, I thought the gentleman would have learned a thing or two by now. Still chasing actresses?' Then he pointed out the way to the garden. 'You'll pass three inns on the way. Turn up the lane after the fourth.'

There was the hillside and there indeed was the old garden, white with snow, a stout old matron playing the virgin. The miserly trees hide their thinning twigs under shrouds of snow, the bushes are bare and old before their time, the scrupulously clean snow-covered paths are patterned with footprints of foxes, rabbits and other innocent visitors. It is as if summer had never been – no lawn, no shrubbery, no lush overarching boughs. As if no one had ever wandered down these winding paths, no one from the old castle, no pink-faced courtiers with ladies on their arms (ladies in deerskin boots!), no one from the little town below, no seamstresses hanging on to excitable young students, no frightened but happy girls making their way to forbidden secret rendezvous with men waiting and twirling their moustaches under the chapel arches; no one at all except rabbits and more rabbits.

Everything was silent and pure and virginal, only an old rook flapped its black wings and trailed its brown shadow across the snow. Sindbad proceeded quietly, looking left and right, but the garden seemed empty, the ruins and the snow presenting a picture of eternal decay.

Then a dark shadow appeared from behind the castle. It was a woman in a long coat, with a little eagle-feathered cap on her head, eating something, dipping her fingers into a brown paper package. As soon as she saw Sindbad she hastened to stuff this into her handbag.

'It's Paula,' thought Sindbad and began to walk rapidly towards her, while she stood chilled and motionless, and perhaps a little scared, in the middle of the path. There was anxiety written across her heart-shaped face, and her deep brown eyes fixed Sindbad with an almost tearful look of entreaty. Then suddenly she brightened and a timid, hopeful smile transformed her whole expression: it was as if two fireflies had raised their wings in the pupils of her eyes. One foot advanced from beneath the long coat and she took a step forward.

'Good heavens, what are you doing here?' she cried, looking him up and down.

Sindbad seized her hand, squeezed it, kissed her glove, then took her chin in his hand and gazed deep into that suffering and gently fading face which was the colour of pressed flowers. 'Weren't you waiting for me?' Sindbad asked. 'Didn't you dream with me?'

'I did dream once, last week or maybe it was yesterday. But I dream a lot of foolish things. I remember now: we were acting something together on stage and you, sir, were wearing a frock-coat with a big star on the left lapel. How did you get here?'

'I dreamt you were dreaming with me, so I set out.'

'You always had a ready way with words,' answered the actress with a faint suppressed laugh.

'I began to wonder what you were doing, and about your life in general since we last met. It's a year now. Remember? We were cruising down the Danube, the stars were shining and the trees were thick on the shore. The captain was Serbian. He was in love with you.'

'Joco.'

'Not unrewarded, I trust? …'

'What do you think I am … I never saw him after that. After all I was yours then.'

'I loved you very much.'

Paula bowed her head a little and stared at the snow. 'Happy creature, how easy it is for you to say that. If only we poor women could afford to say such things!'

'I'm here. Isn't that enough? I've come to you because I wanted to kiss your hand. Let me look at you. Turn around. Let me examine you from head to foot. Hm. You've not changed at all.'

'I am often unwell.'

'Your figure is as it was, neat and graceful ... Let me smell your hair! Show me your shoes and your stockings! You ought to wear finer gloves. The little ribbon about your neck is charming.'

'No one takes any notice of me.'

'You have no sweetheart?'

The actress half-closed her eyes, then, suddenly maternal, stroked Sindbad's arm. 'You fool. Do you think it was so easy to forget you?'

'Snake in the grass!' cried Sindbad silently to himself. 'Liar! You have forgotten me often enough!' But still he liked Paula touching him, it satisfied something in his heart to see the laced shoes, the fresh floral band and the light stockings of the woman for whose sake he had once sailed down the Danube all the way to Pancsova.* The smell of her hair was as delicious as the scent of brushwood tucked into the folds of clean underwear and the almost invisible lines on her face, like the marks of tiny scuffling birds' feet, made him feel sad and affectionate at the same time. It was as if she had spent sleepless nights lost in fantasies of which these faint rings round the eyes were the silent evidence. Sindbad could still see the trace left by his kiss on the fading velvet of her lips: amorous farm-girls' bodies left just such marks among the meadow flowers, their contours still apparent on the crushed lawn. The white neck which craned so curiously from the black dress was like a bird's neck twinkling under the black velvet ribbon, the pocket of her coat was warm and lined with cat fur and made a little nest into which Sindbad slid his hand to find hers.

'I have a wonderful idea for this afternoon,' said the actress, her shoulders brushing against Sindbad's chest. 'Come to the cellar with us. Kápolnai – an old local teacher – has invited members of the company into his cellars this afternoon. His wine is good and the cellar itself is very neatly arranged. I'll make sure the old teacher invites you.'

'I'll be at the café this afternoon.'

'Good, we'll come for you there. Now please be good enough to escort me home. I live not far from here.'

Sindbad was still lost in thought behind the mallow-coloured curtains of the café, when the teacher, a grey-haired, red-cheeked, croaky-voiced old fellow, clattered in, embraced him, told Sindbad that he was to regard him as his best friend, and assured him of a choice pipe back in his cellar. 'Hurry now! Quickly!' he cried heartily. 'There's an awful lot of snow between here and the cellar.'

The company of players was waiting at the café door, mostly cheerful ragged juveniles and two women, Paula and the singer, a plumpish blonde who immediately fixed Sindbad with a searching look as if to say, I know what you've come here for. Pápai the prompter was puffing his pipe at the back of the group, reading a theatrical magazine as if this had nothing at all to do with him.

'Come along, class!' commanded the teacher good-humouredly and reached into his coat where the cellar keys were jangling. 'It's lovely to be together again.'

On leaving town and turning into a narrow winding lane which led up the hillside they suddenly came upon a huge snowdrift. But even from here they could see the soot-coloured entrance to the cellar and with a lot of cheering and shouting the young actors set out across the snow-covered meadow.

'Hurry up!' the old teacher encouraged them.

Happy and proud, Paula snuggled against Sindbad's shoulder and clung to his arm. 'Help me, Sindbad,' she whispered.

Pápai brought up the rear and yelled out at them. 'Can't wait till dark, eh! There's no softer mattress in the world than fresh fallen snow!'

'The nerve of the man!' Paula complained with a soft throaty laugh.

Sindbad saw the high, soft field of virginal snow and had to admit the old prompter was right.

The Secret Room

There once was a woman who kept Sindbad prisoner for almost a year and a half and afterwards he could never erase it from his mind. She was called Artemisia and she was the wife of a landowner whose estates consisted chiefly of forest in a district where bushy-bearded priests presided over Mass and the eyes of the baby Jesus were made of precious stones. A crow was perched on top of the snow-covered tower, perhaps the very same crow he saw through the high barred windows of the thick masonry wall when he was a prisoner of the lovely Artemisia. The secret room where Sindbad spent his year and half in the highlands was in an area where men had long ago raised walls and dug secret passages which extended through the house and the surrounding countryside: in the previous generation there had been another man imprisoned there, but then it was Artemisia's mother who had held the keys. On the peeling wall above the settle a German poem was still visible. The previous inhabitant had written it in his boredom. The inside of the wardrobe door was covered with various other inscriptions that Sindbad's predecessor had absent-mindedly scribbled while changing his shirt. An itinerant Romeo had lived here – in those days there were still such people about – and the constabulary was after him for dealing in false currency and cardsharping. Artemisia's mother concealed the fugitive, persuaded herself that he was a patriot republican in hiding, and soon had the then master of the house, a man not in the first flush of youth, nodding with satisfaction that it was no longer he who had to occupy this secret room, which often remained without heating the whole of the winter thanks to the hard-heartedness of the aforementioned lady ... Sindbad often had to bite his knuckles to prevent himself laughing when he thought of these strict and miserly women who beat their husbands while putting themselves at the service of equally vehement lovers, checking that their maidservants were safely tucked up in bed before tiptoeing through the garden gate, out into the night ...

Who is living in the secret room now? wondered Sindbad one day when, like most prisoners, he felt like revisiting that place with strong towers and high walls where he himself had once been chained up ... So Sindbad set out hoping that at last he might be able to gaze calmly into the eyes of the maid of whom he had been so frightened at one time that he hardly dared speak to her without clasping his hands in prayer. 'How come I never once kicked her!' thought Sindbad, grinding his teeth.

It was night and the snow shone as it usually did in those highland towns where you can see the bells in the belfry a long way off and can make out with surprising precision the shadowy figure who begins to toll them at midnight. Near the river the blue-dye man* was painting the snow ashen grey, apparently trying out a new colour for use on Slovakian girls' skirts. Everyone in town was fast asleep, the snores of the bushy-bearded magistrate resounded right through the market-place, young women slept under Christmas trees together with their children, and the old ones dreamt of tales told during the evening, in which, on snowy nights, pitiless bands of men from far-off countries would overrun the little town and seize the women from right under the Christmas trees.

Naturally, Sindbad was familiar with their dreams, since the dead know everything, but he did not hesitate on his way to the brown gates built into the wall from which spiral stairs lead up to the first floor which remains dark, even by day, and the Christmas tree stands in the front room with its nuts and almonds and scent of gingerbread and the women are sleeping under it on home-made rugs. At the opposite corner a rust-coloured iron door protected the inner recesses of the house, a house with frozen eaves and frosted windows, which in the bright night looked like a house cut out of paper, the chimneys hovering pale blue against the sky and a white curtain trembled in one of the windows as Sindbad silently crept into the house. The night-watchman was just making his way through the deep snow down the high road – he seemed to be alarmed by the shadows of the houses – and caught a glimpse of a queer little patch of luminous fog before him, like light flashing off a helmet or a sword.

Artemisia was sitting before her mirror examining her reflection. This had become her usual practice at night since she had reached the age of forty some time ago and still could not get enough of the lies men told her. She bound her jaw firmly against wrinkles, as people do with the dead, and desperately brushed her hair and braided it without ever taking her eyes off the mirror in the hope of seeing there, just once, the face she used to see, her bygone beauty peeping out from under the mask of the present. One day, the melancholy, frowning, discontented shadow would vanish from those bright leaves of glass, and she, the White Woman of Lőcse,* to whom eligible young men had told long streams of lies, would enter the fortress gate and move quietly forward to reassume her place. Sadly, the shadow remained unaltered, however much she braided her hair or rubbed colour into her cheeks with a rabbit's foot. The wardrobe full of white garments reached to the ceiling and the locks clicked as solemnly as the fortress gates while Artemisia sought for her night-clothes in the drawer. A small mirror hung on the wardrobe door – someone had won it at a fair – looking in it now she discovered Sindbad standing at her shoulder.

'What a surprise!' she cried out. Then with a sweet and most affectionate smile she raised the candle to Sindbad's face.

'You've grown old. Time passes. Whatever happened to you? Whose feet are you kneeling at now? Has one of my immoral old friends consented to adopt you as her *cavalier servente*? It must be that little brunette you told stories to the afternoon you begged me to bring her to you? Do you remember you were telling her about the black-scarved girls of Venice. Oh, how you've aged.'

Sindbad smiled patiently at her. 'And if you could see yourself, you poor thing. When I was a boy I fell in love with a village girl. She was sent to the city where she could learn sewing and stitching. She was away for half a year. By the time she returned her face was ruined by cheap paint, her hair was dyed green and yellow and some of her teeth were gone. Much like you, poor thing,' Sindbad thought to himself and tried not to look at her shoulders, her neck, and under her arms since she had just raised an arm and her sleeves had slipped back.

'I remember this dress,' murmured Sindbad with a tired indifference. 'It is the one you wore when you tried to kill yourself. You had tied the string around your neck and knelt down under the door-handle. I happened to come in at that moment.'

'Nonsense!' she exclaimed. 'I saw you coming across the market square, after you had left me and escaped. I had written to you, asking you to visit me one last time. That is when the little incident with the string occurred. If this doesn't work, I thought, I will give you up.'

Sindbad gazed thoughtfully into the woman's eyes. 'Did you really think, my dear lady, that I would believe in this so-called suicide? ...'

'Heaven knows,' Artemisia answered with bowed head. 'Men are idiots and will believe anything. Even that a woman would kill herself for a man's sake. Every attempt at suicide begins as a joke or a game. There are times the door fails to open in time, or the gun happens to go off ... What woman would be fool enough to die for a man?'

Sindbad laughed silently. In that case he was perfectly justified in leaving the women he had seduced without the slightest pang of conscience ... Were not all women alike? With the passage of time, after a little loving, they were all the same. Their wicked little natures, their contempt for some ridiculed suitor, their defences against laughable sentimentality: eventually they were always driven to name-calling and mockery. In old age they talk slightingly of the grandly moustached suitor in his yellow boots, and make particular remarks on the amusing appearance of the visiting stranger who meant everything to them and for whom they would have given their lives at the time.

'You might care to remember, Sindbad, that on the day of my so-called suicide I spent the night at a ball where I had a wonderful time, staying till well into the morning. It was the miners' ball and the hall was filled with the scent of hot punch which clung to everything, from the mirrors' scarlet hangings to the men's mouths. The snow came down in drifts throughout the night and the roads were buried under it. It was impossible to get home in my delicate little dancing shoes. A kind young man volunteered to carry me home in his arms across the market square. My poor old husband was left stumbling behind with his lantern and bunch of keys. I caught a glimpse of myself in the confectioner's window. I looked rather pretty in my pink ball gown ...'

'And the secret room?' enquired the night visitor.

'The secret room soon had a new lodger. Neither my heart nor the room were ever empty of lodgers. I never could live without love. It was only yesterday, or the day before, that the most recent tenant left, a half-crazy violinist. The room is vacant. If Mr Sindbad has nothing better to do he could take up his old residence,' answered Artemisia.

Sindbad looked away. 'Strange, how while I was lying in my grave I believed that because I had suffered greatly for your sake and finally put an end to my own life you would remain true to my memory. You were nearing forty when I left you.'

'A woman's age does not count, my dear.'

'I loved you, I burned for you, I was a slave to you. I thought no one could whisper such lovely eloquent words in your ear as I did, I, who practically died in an ecstasy of happiness whenever I was in your company.'

'A red-bearded mercenary soldier arrived in town,' muttered the woman. 'A caveman, who dragged me around by the hair ... Will you not take up your old quarters, Sindbad? Lord, how you have aged!'

Sindbad didn't answer. He was bored. And recognising this he left the house in which he had spent a year and a half slaving and suffering in the most delightful way.

Escape from Women

H ere begins the last tale of the voyager which young girls and young men may read, questioning perhaps a detail here and there. In time they too will encounter those miracles which remain wholly unsuspected in one's youth: the miracle of the inexpressible goodness of women as they sit on their beds combing out their long hair, speaking to their lovers with such ardour and selfless devotion that the lovers believe themselves loved for ever; and the miracle of the treachery of women when a man can only clench his fist, seize a knife, load a revolver, wake with bloodshot eyes, or chew in despair on his own tear-drenched pillow.

Dead as he was, Sindbad was often astonished to recall that he had never once killed a woman. As his carriage entered that region where the power of women no longer extends, he looked back and saw mostly pious charitable women in his wake.

'The strange thing,' he thought to himself, 'is that women tend to behave better than one has a right to expect. Poor things, giving their all, their kisses, their dreams and sighs, smuggling my name into their evening prayers – I'd be surprised if the angels didn't wonder

at times what my name was doing among the usual
company of aged fathers, mothers and tiny children ...
They were very good indeed, poor creatures. From now
on Sindbad will teach the young to cherish women, as
they do flowers, as indeed they do so many odd, weak,
cheated, robbed, often tortured beings ... Is it not touching that for all the times they have been disappointed,
the hours they have wept and mourned, nothing con-
tinues to engage them so intensely as the serious subject
of love. Love is everything to them: the air they breathe,
the water they thirst for, the miracle they marvel at. They
talk of love as though it were something that had inde-
pendent existence, something so solid it might be
grasped. Though it is true that the subject of fashion runs
a close second to love in their thoughts.

'God bless you then, dear good women – virgins,
countesses, women of affairs, half-crazed Jewesses* –
all who listened with trembling lips, sceptical smiles
and with desire and astonishment in your hearts when
Sindbad favoured you with softly spoken, delicately
enunciated lies that filled your heads and souls, that
heightened your colour and your mood, and gave you
something to think about ... For his part, Sindbad would
go on to leap from the windows of cursed castles and
cry his eyes out for some other woman. At other times,
in a complete daze, wholly undiscriminating, he would
reach out to pluck one of you, almost anyone – a tea-rose
or a roadside thistle – and would have forgotten your
name by the morning. Forgotten names and voices,
voices into which whole lives were poured, your endless
self-sacrifice, the dangers into which your passions led

you, and the peculiar, precious vows which Sindbad managed to extract from you with the skill of a practised father-confessor – all forgotten. You were all happy to forswear yourselves in the hour of love … Really it hardly mattered that not one of you ever kept her vow. And, oh, how often you offered up your jewels, your influence, the remainder of your lives.'

'Until tomorrow,' one would say as Sindbad was packing his bags.

'I'll bring pictures of the children next time,' a second promised even as another woman was waiting at some other port of call.

'Now we shall never leave each other,' ventured a third.

The sails were already fixed and Sindbad was only waiting for a favourable wind.

What was it they loved?

They liked to be treated well. One should treat the majority of well-disposed females with tenderness, as one would treat a child, approving all their nonsense, greeting each petty remark with delight and noticing each new dress, lavishing praise on the most incidental of new accessories. Do so and your fortune's made. What is most astonishing is that it is the cleverest of them, those hard-headed professional women, who are the readiest to announce that a man has been wholly captivated by their latest item of footwear!

They liked fine words. They liked music, flowers, sentimental promenades, hours filled with tears, painful farewells; they liked any event, however minor, however common, which could stop the clocks of routine even for a minute.

They liked gestures of self-sacrifice. It is a well-known fact that many women take it as a personal insult if the suitor does not threaten to hang himself from the tree beneath her window. And wealthy women are almost more demanding of little presents than the poor ones who need them. An extremely rich woman once told her lover at their first appointment: 'What are you to me? My benefactor. Have you bought me anything yet?' And yet this lady was so respectable and good that all the orphans in town would kiss her hand, and her heart was known to be of such pure gold that it was doubtful whether the jewellery shops of heaven had ever produced anything finer.

They liked the word *fiancé* and they liked the word *lover* – they liked to form lifelong relationships at the first meeting and one may be perfectly sure they never seriously thought that love might eventually end. They liked long eloquent letters – and though they frequently did not read them right through they felt insulted if the letter did not look long enough. They liked it when men collected mementos such as locks of hair, garters, hand-kerchiefs, prayer books, hairpins, shoes, anklets, rings, little slips of paper, railway tickets, dying flowers, pieces of ribbon, leaves of trees with pleasant associa-tions, veils, horseshoe nails (if these were found in pairs), portraits, coins, crumbs from cakes, pebbles, cigarette ends, buttons, shirts, books, strings of corsets and empty matchboxes. There was one woman who was especially kind to Sindbad and trusted him with the

management of her estate, accepted his advice on finan-
cial matters, gave him her jewellery for safe-keeping
and even entrusted him with documents relating to her
divorce. At the end of the affair she asked for no bills
but that he should return to her a particular number of
the evening paper, *Az Est*, which she had had in her
possession in the course of a railway journey between
Vienna and Budapest and in the margins of which this
elegant lady had drawn curious little pictures such as
street children chalk on the walls of houses. She was
anxious and unhappy and unable to sleep till the old
newspaper was found. 'See how much I loved you!' she
said with a pained expression and put it to the flame of
the candle until it lay in a thousand blackened pieces on
the floor.

They liked domesticity. Once Sindbad brought great
joy to a very dear lady when he learned from her the art
of knitting stockings. Other women radiated happiness
when Sindbad knocked a nail into the wall as a picture
hook, when he mended a lock in the house, or when, in
the course of a stay at some village, he rose early to
check that things at the mill were proceeding as they
should. There were ladies among his old acquaintance
who forgave Sindbad anything providing our mariner
ran down to the butcher to buy a few crowns' worth of
smoked meat to supplement an already ample supper.
Others kept him locked up quietly and secretly on the
ground floor while they slept content on the floor above.
There are ugly snub-nosed men who owe their good
fortune to their ability to deal with a horse at stud. It is
particularly the women who have experienced the love

of handsome and refined gentlemen when young who seem happiest to accommodate some slight disfigurement in a man's nose or other bodily part in later years.

And they liked order. They liked to keep track of all Sindbad's debts and to frown and fret over the means of clearing them. 'You'll see how good it is once your mind is at rest,' they'd say, especially older women who tried to persuade Sindbad that their love for him was purely Platonic. Ah, these Platonic affairs afforded Sindbad hearty amusement. He bowed his head, smiled to himself, and waited quietly to see what the women wanted of him. They forbade him wine, cards and loose company, kept his underwear in order, and were delighted when he pretended to feel drowsy at dusk. How often did they make him swear to abjure dice and to drink wine only by small glassfuls! Sindbad could repeat every form of vow by now, word for word; he knelt down without being asked and was delighted to get through the ordeal. For the next few days he would feel very well, covering the woman's hands with grateful kisses, checking over her book-keeping and quibbling with the taxman over a few pennies, then he'd disappear without warning.

He had been loved by blondes, brunettes, slim girls and fat ones, and each time he believed he had found his one true love, just as they believed they had found theirs and never forgot him.

As the years went by there were messages from far away. Women wanted him to come back: they were bored, they felt nostalgic; they wanted to laugh, cry, cackle, fret and be happy. But Sindbad did not go back because he kept account of the lovers that had succeeded him in their affections. The subsequent pain and bitter disappointment prevented him ever forgiving their unfaithfulness. He was a rogue: in the Middle Ages he would have gone the rounds of the prisons where he would have been shorn, first of his nose, then of his ears. Furthermore, he always believed he was speaking the truth and one can ask no clearer proof of a man's wickedness. He could never forgive women. He thought he perceived miraculous qualities in them, a combination of the fidelity of the saints with the virtues of the martyrs. And how he would rage when one of them took up with another man though it was he who had done the leaving.

Let us therefore close the file on Sindbad's not altogether pointless and occasionally amusing existence.

Mrs Bánati, the Lost Woman

W here does the story of Mrs Bánati begin? Where does it end? Perhaps it begins like the river's source, springing from the earth in little runnels. Somebody is playing a thin-toned violin at the window and Mrs Bánati is still in pigtails, looking in the mirror and listening to the violin. The river gathers force and shoulders its way past cities and towers, past ever-fresh landscapes; morning finds it at a well-kept park, by the evening it is washing the banks of a cemetery or toying with the lanterns of the great city. The thin-toned violin has fallen quiet and big-chested men are looking deep into Mrs Bánati's eyes: one man declaims at her as he might at some public meeting, another sighs and murmurs lovely words at her, and a third hides his intentions under a little black silk cap and keeps repeating how he wishes only to console her, regale her with good advice and make life comfortable for her but never notices what shoes she is wearing. Men come and go like landscapes along a river. Following her fourth marriage Mrs Bánati was engaged in reflecting on the lies told her by men – reflecting on how things were, for no one was currently lying to her. At night the shades of discarded men visited her and sat down beside her but Mrs Bánati peevishly hid her face in the pillow.

'You're all the same – you all said the same things with the same intent, now you can all leave me in peace.'

It was at this time, one autumn night – just as the bloodshot moon was sitting like a tipsy old man in the branches of the poplar tree, when all manner of intangible shadows flitted from garden to garden so that it seemed as if night was spontaneously producing animal and vegetable forms of its own, when faithful likenesses rendered in oils grew bored of leaning all day on their frames and stepped out into deserted rooms, when the stories of Kisfaludy* trembled on the tables of old houses and the pages turned over by themselves, when clocks that no one could remember working began to move their hands, and when doors on unoccupied floors of occupied houses started creaking as if in pain because someone behind them dared not cross the threshold – it was then that Sindbad rose from the dead. On this very autumn night he, the enchanted mariner, was driving down the highway in a carriage whose wheels were made of fallen poplar leaves.

The house, which might just as well have been a castle, lay between a high stone wall and dreaming lime trees, like something out of a novel Sindbad might have read in his youth. Although the house, as I have already said, looked innocent enough from the outside, Sindbad brought his hearse to a stop and, having hung the lid of his coffin on a roadside scarecrow and propped up the straw-hatted and green tail-coated figure in the driver's box, slipped quickly through the keyhole of the gate.

Assuming a cloak composed of the damp mist rolling about the garden, he settled on the window, entered, snapped a rusty string in the piano and, looking in one of the locked drawers, found, together with a bottle of hair dye, an old dance card, an autographed fan, an ancient rabbit's foot and a faded love-letter, the little twist of hair which Mrs Bánati had long ago woven out of one of Sindbad's locks and which she had vowed to wear forever next to her heart.

'It's been years since we last met!' Sindbad whispered into the sleeping woman's ear, which lacked the oriental gold earring which used to dangle so enticingly beside her own golden ringlets.

Mrs Bánati opened her eyes and quietly waved the apparition away. 'Let me sleep, Sindbad. I was just dreaming of my first husband.'

Sindbad chortled lightly, like the wild dove in the middle of the wood. 'The first? I remember him: Jeney the photographer, who was later charged with fraud, took a picture of him in the damp little alley near the Greek Orthodox church. There he stood like some returning emigré, leaning on the low gate that used to be at the end of the garden, with his great thick beard and that fancy national costume, staring surprised and anxious into the black tube, behind which the tiny Jeney, with his mousy moustache was twiddling with shutters under the green cloth ...'

'He used to call me Liska,'* Mrs Bánati told her pillow as if there were no one else in the room with her. 'There was an old woman somewhere from whom he hoped to inherit something. It was her name. One day he fell from the roof while he was trying to mend the thatch he had tied himself. I don't remember any more about him.' She gave a quiet sigh. 'He was a good man ...'

Sindbad laughed as uproariously as the devil in the lane by the ditch when a gypsy wedding is in progress at the far end of town and the violinists, cellists and clarinettists are making their loud way home ... 'A pale half-crazy musician lived in town, a long-haired lanky thing, who played "Demon Robert" with a passion and all the windows in town opened when he did so – do you remember him?'

'They called him Sindbad,' answered the woman and dreaming, blushed. 'My dear good husband was laid out on the bier wearing the national costume he had arranged to be photographed in, with the neighbouring women busily combing out his beard. It was evening and the musician came to pay his respects to the dead. The candles looked like dying suns and an old walking stick with leather tassels was leaning in the corner of the room like a trusty friend: I could have frightened the musician away with it but didn't, though I felt my husband's presence so powerfully I thought I would only have to call him and he would wake. My second husband beat me a great deal. He was a soldier. He carried a whip.'

The night visitor stroked the woman's hand. 'I know. You were always complaining about it. I was quite ready to believe the story, but I never found a mark on your shoulder.'

'He was coarse,' the woman defended herself. 'That's why I turned Calvinist, so we could divorce according to the laws as they were. Unfortunately, the minister of the new church I attended on Sundays never managed to preach a sermon that was to my taste. That might be why my third marriage turned out so unhappily.'

'Madam, you have walked the earth in many guises. When you were a girl you wrote in your diary that you would choose to be a woman of pleasure because the poet Reviczky, whom you adored, had composed some of his finest verses about them. Then came the musicians with their treble clefs, their violins wrapped in green broadcloth, piccolos in pockets, nights of meditation, dreams of old deserted gardens, the wind gently tinkling the wind-chimes. Hunchbacks, asthmatics, consumptives – musicians all. One taught you to catch pneumonia by crossing the snow-covered yard at night in bare feet; another to weep on the stool by the glazed door with the green curtains; a third lured you into churches where, at a wave from the conductor, the timpanist would practically raise the roof with his pounding, and in the silence that followed the soprano would bring a new calm, and a man in one of the side-altars would shoot himself for love of you … As soon as the musicians had gone there appeared a drunkard with wild hair who had never been a soldier but succeeded in trampling through your heart in his great spurred boots. What riotous duets you would sing together when you were in drink.'

'Bankruptcy was staring us in the face for the third time. I was in continual fear of starving to death. My husband brought no money in, but spent his time at the card table with an old torn Swiss pack in his pocket instead of my portrait. And I was only thirty-six at the time. I used to stand at the window night after night, waiting for him ... That's when I got to know the night sky and understood why the stars at dawn look as if they have been weeping.'

'There was a scholar living in the area at the time who used to stare at the same stars when he tired of studying ...'

'That's a lie!' Mrs Bánati proclaimed passionately. 'I swear my whole life has been one round of unhappiness. I swear I suffered sleepless nights, I swear on the life of my fourth husband who joined the army, poor thing. I swear I never ...'

'Sindbad was the scholar's name,' whispered the night shadow. 'You must have been happy with someone.'

'Only with the first,' gushed Mrs Bánati. 'He was my true love, the sweet darling ... Mind you, if the present one were to return at last from the war ... Perhaps he is the best after all.'

Sindbad kissed the lady's hand and the cockerel beneath the window began to crow. 'If I pass this way again I might call in.' And he left as silently as he came.

He shoved the old scarecrow into the driver's seat so he could resume his old place in the coffin. 'The hotel, and be quick,' he ordered.

The Green Veil

he body of St Ladislas being carried on a wagon,*
says the ancient script under a painted window in
the Matthias Church* and one afternoon at the
altar, under the icon of the canonised king, while the
wife of the steward was dozing at the gates with her keys
in her lap, and some of the black-clad women of Buda
were seated at a considerable distance from each other
in the pews, like the clubs on a pack of French cards,
each preoccupied with her own troubles and prayers,
that old rake Sindbad was busily eliciting a promise of
eternal love. He was proceeding according to an ancient
rubric which ordained that he should lure his female
acquaintance into empty churches of a quiet afternoon,
and recount to them, in hushed but clearly comprehen-
sible tones, the histories of the various saints depicted
in the building. Jewish women would be enticed to
kneel on a hassock at the tomb of King Béla* and his
queen, the very hassock on which the queen herself
used to pray, then Sindbad would touch their brows
with consecrated water and, later, in the choir or in some
other quiet corner of the church, extort a long passionate
kiss from them. Those less willing would be admonished: 'Please don't cry out, respect the sanctity of the

church.' Women were loth to resist him in old churches,
particularly non-Catholic women; they were overawed
by the wonderful altarpieces, by the odour of sanctity
drifting above them, by those mysterious pointed windows against which the prayers of dead kings still
seemed to flutter like the wings of doves, by the smoke
of the censers, and by those hidden nooks and crannies
in which, come dusk, some prince of hitherto unspotted
virtue might come to life and tug at their pigtails with
his iron-gauntleted hands. The steps leading to that altar
had been trodden by bishops in velvet slippers. How is
one's heart to remain unaffected by the knowledge that
the earnest prayers of men and women had fluttered
from their souls like tiny butterflies compounded of
sighs, and were even now covering the columns and
vaults above so that barely a pinhead of vacant space
remained between them? And who knows whether at
night, with only the eternal flame to light them, those
prayer-butterflies might not come to life and drift down
the aisles as if the air were a powdered spectrum, rising
and falling, a strange snow reflecting the colours of the
altar-candle. Prayers might interlink there: the prayers
of brothers embrace, the sighs of lovers settle beside
each other, so when the first rays of the sun descended
through the windows they might be the first to rise into
the highest regions together. Perhaps only the prayers
of happy children frolicked in the highest regions in the
moonlight beneath the vaulting; the prayers of old virgins, liverish and crazed old women's fantasies, might
flap on bat wings below them, though their prayers
could sometimes be as yielding as Persian rugs, since it

is old women who have the most beautiful dreams of unknown men. Silky as moths, whiskery, covered in pollen, the thoughts of mature women fluttered beyond individual lovers on the lightest of wings, while the choir filled with grim, retiring, crook-beaked birds waiting for dawn when they might steal silver and gold coins from the sky. It was here that Sindbad made Mitra swear eternal love to him. Then he took her by the arm and, deeply moved, led her from the church.

'From this day on I shall regard you as my wife,' Sindbad told her in the Biedermeier café where the lovers of Buda tended to stop for refreshment.

Mitra nodded sadly. 'I feel God will punish me for it. You have seduced and ruined me. I don't know how I can face my old parents again. They worship a different God.'

'There is only one God,' proclaimed Sindbad with conviction, 'He who lives in our hearts and is born out of our love. It is the God who protects us, who allows us to meet in secret, so that no one should know of our love; who tells me what you think; who takes care that our eyes should seek only each other's, who joins our hands, and brings our hearts together like two tempest-tossed birds that have found each other ...'

'You believe in love?' asked Mitra, gazing at him with big round eyes.

'I believe in nothing but love. Almost everything that exists exists only because men and women love each other. I may be old-fashioned, but in my experience, even today, men spend a great deal of time gazing into women's eyes. Take this place – this old café only exists because lovers choose to meet here. The tables are made so that feet may freely touch, hands clutch unobtrusively and faces approach so close that, come April, you can see the first freckles of spring on a woman's cheek. Think of the desire and passion stirring in those who have worn these chairs smooth with their young bodies. Shoes that used lightly to tap each other are now lying discarded on the rubbish heap in St Lawrence's yard, and gloves, drawn off so that bare fingers might touch each other, when to draw those gloves off was a matter of such life-shattering importance – where are they now? The words 'I love you' have been said as often in this little shop as the bells of the great tower in the city have rung out over the Danube. Women and men have sat here, looking at each other, desiring each other, and not one has asked, as you have, madam, if I believed in love.'

'My convent school, my books, the warning terrifying voices of my parents, all tell me that love is an awful unpleasantness. My friends would all laugh at me if they knew I had sworn eternal fealty to you. Why? Because I don't love you. I don't even know what it is to love,' answered Mitra, whom Sindbad had by a long and painful process succeeded in persuading to come to Buda, to walk with him, to have her confess her love to him, to gaze from the battlements of the Bastion over the Field of Blood, and to linger in the royal gardens.

She was a lively dark-eyed girl who often prayed at home with her aged parents, and was unhappy at always having to listen to business affairs at the table. Sindbad spent days under her window, performing all kinds of tricks with his grey hat, making friends with the grocer, the coalman, the stall-holder on the corner – even the policeman greeted him as he strode along the pavement before Mitra's house. It took Sindbad a long time to make the girl's acquaintance, having collected all his lies and displayed them to her like a shopkeeper putting his most glittering wares in the window. Mitra listened to his sweet talk with a serious and contemplative expression. 'A refined and corrupt man,' she once called him. She was eighteen already and had few illusions.

'Do you remember Esther, about whom Baron Miklós Jósika* wrote that novel of his?' Sindbad persevered, and gave her the book the next day. She leafed through it, bored.

One afternoon he lured her to a theatre with his faithful female cronies. Mitra yawned while the music plied her with its seductive rhythms and the dancer danced herself to exhaustion on the stage below.

Then he asked her to draw her curtain one night at a certain time, so she should see him standing stock still in the moonlight, looking like one already dead and returned from the distant shore.

On another occasion, he spent days ignoring her and wore a flower in his buttonhole, one he was given by a notorious vamp in Pest. He wrote a long sorrowful letter. He made preparations to depart for America and placed an antique ring on Mitra's finger.

'Let's go back to the church,' pleaded Sindbad with a solemn and melancholy expression. 'You must rescind the vow you made me at the altar. After all, you weren't serious, nor do you believe in love. I wouldn't want you to carry such a terrible burden on your conscience.'

Mitra shrugged indifferently and followed him, her dancer's ankles twinkling, into the darkening church. A blonde woman in mourning dress was raising her skirt and kneeling before the high altar, just as in *Tosca*. Sindbad nervously grasped the girl's hand.

'Come, you little sinner, beg to be released from your vows and do so now before you tread so far down the path that you become irredeemable. My heart has found peace and lost its ardour. I have forgiven you, but here, between these holy walls, among these saints all worthy of honour, before the eternal flame and in the name of everything the great majority of men regard as sacred and keep hidden within the recesses of their hearts, you must pray to be forgiven your sin. Kneel and pray.'

The canonised king had grown faint on the stained glass, and there was deep silence beneath the vaulting, a silence shared by all those who had prayerfully shed their burdens in this place. Up in the dark heights of the choir a frightened lost bird was clucking to itself.

'Pray,' repeated Sindbad sternly. 'Ask the great king to release you from your vow, redeem your pledge, regain the peace in your soul, find contentment. Beg him devoutly to forget your vows of love, that love which he with his omnipotent hand has created. Ask that neither daughter nor son of yours should suffer unhappiness because of the false vows of others. Pray that you should not love anyone in your life, nor be cheated by anyone the way you have cheated me.'

Having quietly and prayerfully repeated the words of the adventurer, she rose from the altar steps, smiling and lighter of heart. 'How strange I feel,' she said and spread her arms as if seized by some kind of giddiness. 'As I prayed the king's face seemed to disappear and yours slowly took its place. It was Sindbad staring sadly and solemnly at me from the glass as I recited the whole vow. Your immobile face reminded me of an old icon that over the centuries had grown used to hearing the suffering voices of women who have knelt before it, telling of their joys, sorrows and sins. Ah, those saints of old were reliable decent men. They never betrayed anyone. They kept their secrets hidden in the pockets of their coats like passwords. And so, with your permission, secretly, I have added a few words to the prayer, words privy to the icon and my heart.'

The usher's wife was rattling her keys, and the church grew dark in the corner where the queen or beggar-woman used to sit on the low bench. Sindbad drew Mitra closer. 'And what did those silent words say?' he asked quietly.

'If it was really your face on the icon you should have heard them,' answered Mitra, avoiding the question. 'St Ladislas might even now be walking the earth in your likeness.'

'I am indeed St Ladislas,' Sindbad sighed in his vanity. 'That's the nicest thing anyone has said to me this afternoon.'

The goldsmith's daughter gave a quiet laugh. 'What a queer man you are. You believe my vows rather than my eyes, my hands or my voice. Just as you believe the blessed king. There's a dark gateway here. Come kiss me on the lips and give me something to remember the afternoon by.'

And for the first time she raised the green veil from her face.

The Night Visitor

One autumn day Sindbad left the crypt where he had been deposited after his suicide.

He was disappointed to find that the lounge suit he had been so carefully dressed in for his funeral was out of fashion. It might once have been sported by dandies on their daily strolls, but more recently the frock coat had been adopted by schoolteachers and village choir-masters, and as for the britches – Sindbad felt like his own grandfather in them. In those days he used to correspond with village girls and travel to distant and obscure regions in the hope of meeting with different kinds of women. He had a fondness for pointed shoes and the scent of lavender. He also liked Lavalière ties that could be done up in one great bow and white waistcoats cut high, to wear when visiting actresses in the provinces or when asking bourgeois ladies for lockets, handkerchiefs, garters and other *bijou* objects for mementoes. On walks in the Bastion or on visits to the dance school he used to take a deep sniff of their scented dresses and proclaim his love for them without ever once lying; in distracted moods he would dawdle under windows from which, eventually, some attractive woman would lean out; he would bribe chambermaids with a little present and hot-headedly enter strange houses just so that he could kiss the hands of unknown women, beg a blessing off the older ones and extol the virtues of momentary delight, the secret joy, the invaluable fleeting hour, to those who had not previously met him and hence had been taken so utterly by surprise. Ah, life was still worth living then: one might appear secretly by night in a garden, tap at a window, speak beautiful words to those waiting to hear them; one could laugh and grow rapt or languid on the subject of a ringlet, a flower, a small white hand or the peculiar curve of a neck, and watch as the train drew away from the platform. That was Sindbad in his youth – a tireless voyager, a friend to women, a knight errant for those in sleepy provincial towns; he was the last worldly thought of virgins about to enter convents and the hope of the ageing ... When the affair was over he would retreat to the sighing boughs of the damp and melancholy graveyard and spend a whole year listening to the drumming of the rain and, when this too grew tedious, he might engage in conversation with his dead relatives who lay to either side of him in the crypt. One particularly worm-eaten old great-uncle tended to toss and turn in his grave. He had had four wives when alive and two or three lovers beside them at any one time, and was still anxious to reassume the flesh: 'I wonder what my sweet Helen is doing?' he would ask the spiders. 'I died too soon to develop a proper taste for her.'

The restlessness of this girl-crazy uncle would eventually restore Sindbad's appetite for life. One moonlit night, when the sexton left the gates open, Sindbad

escaped from the crypt and set out directly for the place
where he had spent his happiest days.

The old nurse slipped into the house, her cheeks quite
pale, and whispered to her mistress. 'He is standing by
the fence looking into the yard. The moon is shining
directly on him. Would madam like to see him?'

That evening, mistress and maid had happened to be
speaking of Sindbad. They were just remembering the
time when he arrived one night and the fresh snow lay
knee-high in town and the two hands of the illuminated
clock in the tower were standing vertical. They had been
playing cards in the afternoon and the cards slipped
through their fingers with a faint lisp in the silence of
the curtained room. Their very words sounded mysterious.

'There's someone coming to the house, someone
whose thoughts lie here ... Madam will know best who
this person might be ...'

'I don't know,' she answered and her heart beat
faster as she thought of Sindbad. 'You say he is waiting
by the fence?' she asked and her fingers trembled on the
table as she rose.

'I saw him with these old eyes of mine. The neighbour's dogs were fretting and barking,' answered the
old servant.

'Invite him in, Theresa,' said the woman after a few
moments of thought. 'He probably wants to tell me
something.'

The old servant had often kept watch over the dead
at the house: she dressed them, combed their hair,

spoke to them and joined their hands. The employers in whose service she had spent her life had quietly passed away, one by one, like the seasons. She almost had more to do with the other world than with the present one ... She opened the door without thinking. The little gate gave an agonised little creak as if it were more afraid of the dead than she was, then she retired to the kitchen behind the stove.

'Where have you come from?' asked the woman, her face quite white.

The last time Sindbad had passed this way his hair had just begun to grey at the temples, a process as delicate and timid as the uncertain snow that falls in late autumn. Many women had cradled that dear head of his against their bosoms, but it was all winter there now. The frock coat hugged him tightly: he might have been a provincial gentleman on his way to a meeting or to his own silver wedding ... The pointed shoe creaked ceremoniously across the home-made rugs and the folded collar lent a certain dignity to his cleanly shaved chin. A tall cigar case protruded from his cigar pocket. The white waistcoat had probably been dried in the sunlight by careful feminine hands.

'Where have you sprung from? I thought you were dead, I heard you were, but was I dreaming? Why can't you find peace in the other world?' she asked him, as Sindbad sat perfectly still in the soft pointy-legged armchair, having placed his tall hat and dog-skin gloves on the floor like some old dandy.

'I wanted to see you once more, Euphrosyne,'* answered Sindbad, his voice compounded of leaves and shadows. 'I want to talk to you about the bitter past, so full of waiting and hope, about those marvellous days when every morning found us at the window surveying the dawn snow or the brilliant icicles hanging from the eaves in the beautiful beams of the sun peeking over the wooden roofs, when we tried to guess what delights and pleasures the approaching day might hold by gazing at tiny patches of blue sky reflected in pools in the streets. And now I am long dead, I'd like to know how you spend your days, what you are thinking, what you dream of at night. I've come back in the hope that you might welcome a few words of encouragement, advice or reassurance.'

'You're very late,' answered the woman.

Sindbad examined her carefully. Her brow and her eyes, the wavy dark hair swept off her face, the shadow under her long eyelashes: it was all as before. She used to be referred to in town as the Bountiful Mrs Kecsegi; did men still call her that? Only on her temples and in the pallor of her complexion could one detect traces of those sleepless nights and tears shed on the pillow. Many had passed from this house in hearses, to the accompaniment of weeping. Husband, children and lover had one by one left her. Poor woman, her life was an endless round of mourning. And prying, gossipy neighbours do nothing to lighten a widow's load. Perhaps they were already drilling holes in the walls so as to observe the movements of this unattached woman. Who is visiting her in the evening? Who is that she is talking to? Is she really spending her time mourning the dear departed?

'I should take a husband, Sindbad,' the woman apologised and lowered her eyes. 'Next door have drilled a hole in my bedroom wall. They want to pry even into my dreams. I dare not dream any more. I know that once I'm safely married they'll leave me in peace.'

Sindbad reassured her. 'No one can see me, I am only a spirit. Only you can see me, Euphrosyne. I speak to you as if I were a dream figure at your bedside.'

'It's true, when you died I dreamt most intensely of you,' the woman continued, absorbed, as if picking up a long neglected train of thought. It was a persistent thought that accompanied her everywhere, which trailed her, which clung to her dress like some furry little monkey. Sometimes she turned around. Who is following me? 'I dreamt your dead body was laid out on the wood chest in the kitchen and my servants were all dressed in mourning clothes. I picked you up with an enormous effort, and carried you on my shoulders. I almost collapsed under the weight. But I kept going. I took you to bed. I laid you out and kept looking at you to see if you were really dead. You were dead and I strewed the yellow silk eiderdown with flowers … Next day I was sure you were dead. Did I weep over you? I think I wept quietly at night, when no one was looking, when I myself hardly noticed it.'

Sindbad stroked her brow; she felt it like an autumn breeze. 'Ah, you should think of something nicer. Have you revisited the places where we used to stroll arm in arm when no one could see us? Have you walked through those distant suburbs where the houses suddenly shrank so that we could touch their eaves? Have you walked with anyone through an old graveyard where the rain has washed the names off the gravestones and made all the dead anonymous? Have you visited the little pâtisseries where our feet used to touch under the table, or inns where we took shelter for the night, where the innkeeper was as ruddy-cheeked as English novels would have him be, where the windows gave on to a park and we could touch the red leaves of the vine that was growing wild? Have you taken a carriage through the autumn countryside as we used to do, holding hands the whole way, not knowing why? Has anyone told you since I left that your legs are shapelier than the legs of deer on reservations, your hands whiter than those of princesses who have long died and have nothing to do but rest their lovely hands on their heavy silk dresses, that the locks of hair curling on your neck give well-wined and dined young men plenty to think about, and that the rustling of your silk skirt is like the whispering of moss in the forest in June where both happy and unhappy lovers have kissed? Has anyone told you they would die for you and that life without you would be pointless and hopeless?'

The woman sighed and answered in a breaking child-like voice: 'People have said a great deal since then ... But they all lied. Only you told the truth, Sindbad. Oh, how I believed you. I trusted in you as in a god, as in my mother when I was a child. And I have never gone with any other man to those places we visited, where we were constantly telling each other how our love would never end. I have never seen another man's face above my shoulders in the reflection of that lake where we used to row and I would have felt ashamed in front of the old man in the café if, one or two years later, I had waited, hopeful and excited, for an appointment with another man, there where since time immemorial women have waited for their lovers in secret. Will you let me be married again?'

'You have behaved impeccably, so I will,' the ghost answered, pulling his frock coat even closer about him, and ceremonially bending his knee, he gave a little bow and left her.

An Overnight Stay

W hat did Sindbad like?

He liked snowdrifts and women's legs.

The provincial dance school and the little inn where he could sit like a stranger and whisper to the innkeeper's wife, suggesting that they should run away together.

Leaves in the park in autumn, blotched as if with blood, and abandoned windmills where one day he might murder the woman he loved best.

Melancholy roads between the hills and the smile of the woman in charge of the horses at the travelling circus when she received his bouquet.

He liked the scent of graveyard flowers in tales told by old women as they knitted socks and remembered past loves, and the lies he told to novice nuns in the corridors of railway carriages.

He liked wooing complete strangers in highland towns, making up to innocent bourgeois women with many children then suddenly leaving – and peeking through the windows of houses in crooked deserted streets on snowy nights to see what was happening by candlelight.

He liked hands, hair, women's names, voices and caresses. He liked to appear in young girls' dreams, to court fallen women at masked balls as if they were princesses, and to recite poems to those with rough hands.

He liked lies, illusions, fictions and imagination – he would love to have swung from the high trapeze in a rose-pink vest or been an organist at a princely residence, or a confessor in a Jesuit church! A sought-after gynaecologist in Pest or a young tutor in a girls' school! A night-light in the Sacré Coeur, an illuminated capital in the prayer-book when young women are interceding for their dear ones at the Franciscan church! A window pane through which lovers kissed, a tiny icon under the pillow, a silk-ribbon in a high girdle, or a poet in exile whose works were studied by young girls in secret.

Bearing all this in mind it is understandable that the unhappy young man should have taken his own life. His desires were incapable of fulfilment. It was of no consolation to him that one hundred and seven women had reciprocated his love, women who, he imagined, had dandled him into a haze of nostalgia; one hundred and seven women, each of whom had brought something new, irrational but wholly unforgettable into his life: a voice, a gesture, a scent, a strange word, a sigh ... After all, there were more than one hundred and seven women remaining who still haunted his dreams, over one hundred and seven apparitions ringed in red, all of whom he would love to have loved. All of whom he fell in love with at first sight, feeling he had only to extend his hand in order to touch them. When in town, he gazed at women passionately and adoringly, the blood in his temples racing – there were pale flowers on the point of fading, tea-roses ranged along the balconies who looked through him with careless self-conceit, all glowing ears, sweet-scented necks, soft hands and oriental decadence, tight buds and meadow flowers whose fresh lips emitted soft streams of laughter as if they were springs and bubbling brooks, and actresses who had loved often and long. He moaned with the sheer joy of living, his heart in his mouth, every time spring and summer came round and he could watch them parading their new clothes. The white blouses of women about town, the traveller's green skirt and the secretary's cheap shoes; the hair-dresser's black apron, the feathers in the hat of the forty-year-old grand dame, the nurse's white uniform, the black scarf of the impoverished aristocrat from Buda, the actress's loose pantaloons, the hand clad in mother-of-pearl gloves holding opera-glasses in the private box, the leg braced on the high step of the carriage in the process of alighting, the cooing and cackling of Jewish women and the white necks prayer-fully bent in Buda churches; these had occupied Sindbad's imagination throughout his life ... women without their clothes were all the same, they never interested him.

What is more, after his death, whenever the snow flew fast or the wind whistled, and he had occasion to escape from his crypt, he inclined to frequent places which retained some memory of a neatly tied garter or a sweetly sloping shoulder. And his very favourite haunts were those ruined forts, river banks and silent gardens where, enchanted and dizzied by love, he had committed suicide for one or other woman's sake.

In many of his dreams a certain Irma appeared and called to him – she was a woman who lived in a village Sindbad the voyager had once found himself in, in Pest county. The weathercock on the roof had just stopped turning when she saw him step through her narrow gate. The guard dogs had started barking furiously at the moon, and the woman in the inner room had woken up and was listening attentively, her head propped on her elbow.

As Sindbad took a couple of turns about the courtyard it was as if the man in the moon had taken a puff of his long-stemmed pipe and blown a little white cloud of smoke into the moonlit yard. Irma sat up uneasily in her bed and called her old maid who was sleeping in the corner. 'Nana,' said the lady. 'Look out in the yard and see why the dogs are so restless.'

The ancient peasant bumbled over to the window and turned her myopic eyes up to the moon. 'That young man is here again, the one who came before. He's standing by the fence.'

'It's Mr Sindbad, surely,' cried the woman. 'I knew he'd return ... after all, why should he leave me here for ever?'

The maid grunted and sought her bed in the dark. 'He's dead and daren't come in,' she muttered. 'We didn't treat him very well the last time ...'

'It was vintage time, wasn't it?' the woman exclaimed. 'The village was full of the scent of ripe grapes and drunken bees were humming about the terrace. A white-haired gypsy in red breeches was plucking his dulcimer and the roof was dark. The chimney at the end of our house was the only one smoking and there was a great fire in the kitchen. Perhaps the servants were roasting an ox. Mr Sindbad couldn't sleep and was resting his head on the dulcimer, and his strange friend, Joco – we only knew his first name – kept singing one song over and over again in that harsh wine-stained voice of his, like thin ice cracking round a well one winter's day when there's roast pig on the spit and you're chewing a crisp bit of cabbage between your teeth. Like sour wine trickling down an old man's throat, that's what Joco's singing was like, and he had been singing ever since dinner. The weather was really rather mild, it was that lovely time of autumn when the nights are still warm and I was reading poems by Kisfaludy* under the branches of the huge chestnut tree: I was in love with Sindbad. Do you remember, Nana?'

'He was a handsome young man,' the old servant answered with a satisfied grunt.

'The night wore on and on and still they did not move from the terrace. The servant brought more wine: I was tossing and turning in my bed. I heard carnival noises and that voice like broken snow crackling under the sleighs of a wedding party, like the smell of cabbage soup and the taste of bacon hanging in smoky rings, continually singing for Mr Sindbad's entertainment, with the occasional heavy plucking of those thick dulcimer strings. I slipped on my house-shoes and an underskirt and knocked on the window overlooking the corridor. "Stop this noise now." But since Joco had done me the favour of introducing me to Sindbad he was not bound to obey me. He simply raised the bottle of wine in my direction. "What are you so cross about, you little sack of poison?" he mocked me. "After all, I've brought you the man you love." I was so angry I rushed out on to the terrace and knocked the dulcimer over – the whole house vibrated – and I boxed the musician's ear a few times too, but Joco eluded me. I took Sindbad's hand and dragged him off to bed.'

'That's how it was, all right,' sighed the maid.

'It was wonderful!' the woman answered abstractedly and laid her head on her pillow. 'The old dulcimer player has long since died and followed Joco and Sindbad, his partners in festivities, to the grave. Oh, if only I could hear that dulcimer once more and listen to that old song reeking of the beer-hall out on the terrace! If only Sindbad could rest that lovely melancholy head of his in my lap again! If only I could be young once more! And this time I wouldn't box the ears of any musician who was entertaining my darling.'

Far off in the village, the clock in the tower struck twelve, the old count emerged from the church walls, set out for his nightly constitutional and everything began to move: portraits of pig-tailed ancestors and broad-bosomed matrons, thin-lipped women clutching white handkerchiefs; all of them shifted and leaned forward curiously. In the distance one could faintly hear the sound of a dulcimer approaching. Already it was in the neighbouring street and the extraordinary hoarse voice the whole country knew as Joco's sounded as though it were practically next door. People were coming and going under the window, the gates creaked, and suddenly the dulcimer was right there on the terrace among the clusters of wild grapes.

The old maid, lying on her bed, said, 'I have brought them to you, madam. While you were sleeping I slipped out to the cemetery and brought over Mr Sindbad's companions.'

The lady slipped on her house-shoes and crept over to the window. The moonlight had already slid behind the house. The vaulted terrace was dark.

There were shadows perceptible in the faint light of the corridor. Sindbad was resting his head against the dulcimer and Joco, a big-bellied, sharp-moustached, curly-headed old man, was raising a glass of red wine to her. Having greeted her he resumed his singing. The gypsy in red breeches was strumming the instrument with invisible hands. Sindbad bowed his head.

Irma stood at the window, her heart racing. It was only when the ancient cockerel began to crow that she woke from her trance. The shadows were gone from the corridor and the sound of the dulcimer sounded faintly from the graveyard.

Sumach Trees in Blossom

his story begins with Sindbad still a young man –
young in so far as his legs were steady but where
his heart should have been he wore an antique
red-gold amulet rather than a black hole. His eyes
sparkled like the winter sun on frosty pines and his
ankles were so slender and lithe he might have worn
dancing shoes like the professional dancers at The
Green Devil. He gazed mockingly into women's eyes
because he imagined each of them to be a potential
murderer, while all the time his mouth spoke the required words with such refinement and courtesy he
might have been an abbé addressing an innocent elderly
lady who was thinking of leaving her jewellery to the
monastic foundation. He pretty well knew all there was
to know about women's tears, their sighs and inviting
looks, but retained a respect for the sincere hate and fury
they felt when abandoned. Being a wise man, however,
he never imagined that there was a single woman in the
world who spent sleepless nights dreaming passionately
of him. Women were always thinking of something else
when they were alone! At this time, though, he was
inclined to believe that he might deserve a lady's attention.

Here we are thinking of the affair of the goldsmith's wife, who occupied Sindbad's thoughts for some years. Not that he failed to notice that other women possessed neat ankles, fine heads of hair, lovely eyes and attractive voices. Nevertheless, whenever he walked alone under the poplars or idled time away at a small inn in Buda (in the Tabán district* particularly, in those smoke-filled vaulted rooms with large wine glasses where a blind musician wheedled away in a corner accompanying a faded ballad singer and the innkeeper peered so suspiciously out from under his otter-fur cap that he looked as if he were sizing up his chances of passing a bit of counterfeit money) Sindbad carried on dreaming, calculating, setting traps, and contemplating romantic plans for seducing housemaids and countesses. And whenever he was busily planning out his future in this way Sindbad's thoughts invariably centred on the goldsmith's wife: he imagined her in her small château with red windows, its roofs swimming in mist, or saw her riding in a four-horse carriage. In the midst of his reveries, he would often write her name on the table with his finger dipped in wine. The table before him now was covered in large versions of the letter F. The letters together added up to the word *Fanny,* and that word, whether in the smoky, dreamy distance, or in the tops of the poplars or on the yellow walls of the vaulted inn in the Tabán, inevitably conjured the figure of the goldsmith's wife in a wide-collared mantle with a crown on her head like one of those raven-haired Madonnas in some monastery in Holy Russia. The golden amulet Fanny had given him to wear next to his heart showed the Virgin as she might have appeared to pious medieval engravers. Sindbad would often press the relic to his lips when he found himself alone.

Since the goldsmith's wife was very well known in Pest, Sindbad's meetings with her had to be conducted in the most mysterious and exciting secrecy. They met in churches, at balls, at boat races or on the less frequented paths in the sanatorium gardens; in the evening the carriage would wait with curtains drawn in some silent street and the goldsmith's wife would emerge from an alley and on quick delicate feet find the carriage door open and step in; at other times they would exchange stolen kisses on the dark spiral stairs that led to the lame seamstress's shop; or Sindbad would leap on to the streetcar as it entered the tunnel just so that he might secretly squeeze the beloved object's hand for a minute or so; or he would suddenly grasp her arm in the twilit square under the Matthias Church just as the choir was singing the Hungarian 'Hymn to Mary' in the tower.

The happiest times, though, were those they spent in the district through which water used to be drawn up to the castle from the river below, the place still known as Víziváros or Watertown, where the goldsmith's wife had herself been born in a Renaissance-style house. There was a restaurant there which opened in the summer, with sumach trees in the courtyard. These trees changed into a most beautiful red colour as autumn advanced and a red-combed cockerel stood and mused on the unused tables. Red was the wine which the apronned waiter placed before them on the mild end-of-

October afternoon when the wild vine was no longer fruiting on the nitrous walls.

Fanny pointed to the rusty iron-grille marking the floor above them. 'That's where I was born, Sindbad, thirty years ago. My mother died not long after my birth and her polished coffin was carried down the stairs by retired soldiers. My father collected antique boxes and liked to walk about in slippers, and in the evening, once he had finished with his boxes, he'd stand and ponder with his hands thrust into his pockets. My childhood was rather sad on the whole. My best friends were the naked shepherds, the goddesses and the swans, those violinists in powdered wigs and breeches and the enamelled mail coaches which decorated the lids of my father's boxes. Later my father brought home a little old snuff-coloured gentleman who was always reading the fables of La Fontaine. He had a high white waistcoat. I can no longer remember his name but whenever he looked up from the old French book I found I was staring into the most extraordinary, unforgettable pair of eyes I had ever seen. They were sad and blue, all-forgiving, all-comprehending, wise and gentle. They contained everything the house meant to me: patient attention to the tiny joys of life, immediate and tacit forgiveness, good behaviour and the ability to dream quietly. The old Frenchman's eyes taught me to live so quietly as to forget the hustle and bustle of life, that it should be no more than the sound of a small violin being played in a silent street; he taught me that towers may not be known because they are always enveloped in mist, that it is best to suffer unnoticed, that my shoes and gloves should always be clean and that I should comb my brown hair off my neck with a wet comb … When I was first unhappy – many years ago – my instincts led me back to the old house. It was autumn and I sat down at one of these tables and ate cherries and cream. Our old Frenchman was still alive then and he watched me for a while from the corner without my noticing. Ever since then, whenever I'm in trouble, I come here in case the old man is still alive.'

For the first time Sindbad took some trouble to examine the house containing the little summer restaurant which went under the name of The Golden Goose and sported an ancient coat of royal arms above the gate. He noted the red-combed cockerel and the silent gallery above him where the woman he now regarded as his wife used to run about as a child.

One day, after his death, he returned to the house in quiet Víziváros – it was as if he had only left yesterday. The cockerel stood guard in the usual place and the sumach trees waited patiently in their red garments like so many court officials. The elderly royal couple they were waiting for would soon be passing by, their heads bowed, passing by and passing on.

Sindbad didn't have to wait long. He heard light faint footsteps under the arch of the gate. A rusted lock was moaning in the wind, grumbling that though the guard dog was gone human feet were still shuffling, stumbling, struggling and striding down the worn cobbles outside, feet which imagined they were conveying kings, generals, poets and a hundred varieties of happiness home after a night of drinking.

Fanny entered, a sadly bent little wing on her black hat, her veil full of tiny holes the size of snowdrops, and her black-gloved hand as tender and maternal as the precious hands that wipe some minor care from a child's brow. The young man with the blue apron brought some cherries of deep Flanders Red and cream in a little floral cup covered in vine leaves. Someone started playing the violin in one of the upstairs rooms.

Dead Sindbad sat where the old French gentleman might once have sat. He did not cough or make any noise but contentedly watched the progress of a swallow that had flitted across from Pest to Buda. The dead see no change in the living. Dead mothers always return to orphaned children even when their sons have long been wearing beards. Dead fathers, should they awake at midnight, might be found mending the caps of little boys. And, long after they have turned to dry old sticks and firewood, lovers will still be gathering and whispering at the ear of the grey-haired princess, their voices like the sound of wind among the lilacs, their faces young and fresh as they drift by in their red frock-coats and the white waistoats they had worn as musicians. In Sindbad's eyes the goldsmith's wife was as beautiful now as she had been at the masked ball in her youth when he first saw her in her gold embroidered dress in the guise of Maria Stuart.

He sneaked up on her, stealing a ride on a windblown leaf, and began quietly whispering in her ear where her hair smelled fresh and was as neatly combed as if for Sunday. 'My poor darling, are you dissatisfied, miserable, sad?'

'I am very sad because everyone has left me and I'm alone,' the woman sighed to herself. 'I can no longer see the pink-cheeked shepherds I saw in my youth and I no longer hear music on the wind. My lovers are dead or grown old ... Heavens, with what blessed tranquillity I looked forward to strolling quietly and cheerfully along the castle ramparts with some old army officer. Nowadays I can't resign myself to it. Why – because I am no longer young? Why – because I no longer spend the night in tears on account of some unfaithful lover? It is true, I confess, that while they were around I never wept for any of them. Today, though, I would like to cry for all of them, for all their lies, their bad behaviour and fickleness. Not to feel angry but simply to cry, to cry for years, for ever, for them all. How could they leave me without a word? They never even told me why they were leaving. They simply left ...'

'Because their time had come, my poor darling,' Sindbad answered with extraordinary tenderness. 'There is no special reason for men to go. They'd have gone even if you had begged them not to and pursued them or sent messages. Something was calling them, waiting for them, much as the wind calls the leaves. In my case a great storm blew me one night to the window of a poor seamstress ...'

'That is just what is so galling. My pride ...'

Sindbad gave a wicked laugh. 'Your pride? You are proud only as long as you are surrounded by admirers. While you are both conqueror and enchanter.'

The dull tapping of a stick with a rubber end sounded in the deep gateway. A carefully shaven old gentleman in a wing collar and chequered trousers entered the courtyard with the sumach trees and ordered a large glass of red wine.

'Leave me alone, Sindbad. I have no time for your idiotic conversation,' she answered, waving the shadow away.

'I cannot live,' the ghost muttered.

The old gentleman's eyes rolled over her like a beer barrel across a yard. He coughed and hid his stick behind the bench.

'Strange,' sighed the goldsmith's wife. 'Men remain attractive longer than we do. That old gentleman must certainly be the most handsome man in Buda.'

And she adjusted her hat.

Rozina

Sindbad, the bearer of this fine name first found in the volume of *The Thousand and One Nights* our grandmothers used to read, was travelling by train to an appointment with a lady and was lost in his thoughts. He wiped the soot from his face with a little cologne, arranged a new handkerchief in his pocket, rinsed his mouth and checked the tissue paper wrapped around the flowers he had brought from Pest, though he could have bought some locally since the train was due to arrive at the provincial station well before closing time. He lay back then got up again, absent-mindedly started counting the poplar trees as they passed, and wondered whether it was worth his while coming here simply because Rozina was scared of mice.

Having spent winter and spring on Sindbad's arm, kissing, walking the streets of Pest, exploring Buda down hidden byways known only to lovers, and sitting in the boxes of theatres where Sindbad would lean in the shadows behind her, his arms solemnly crossed, Rozina, the goldsmith's wife, avoided the hot summer months by moving to a country house where her grandmother, a veteran of the revolution, occupied herself sweeping the dust and cobwebs from ancestral portraits. 'The quiet life will be good for me. I shall find peace and forget you,' said Rozina on one of their three-mile walks together through the hills of Buda. (Sindbad's eyes were fixed on his feet. It was a long afternoon and his heart was trembling as he wondered whether she would really leave him. In that moment he believed his whole life depended on Rozina, though once she had gone he made a miraculous recovery. He breathed again, a free spirit. 'I'll find a new lover – a dancer!' he thought. Then Rozina unexpectedly sent him an urgent letter. 'Come quickly, I beg you, I can't sleep for the mice.' Sindbad did not think twice, but packed his bags and left.)

There was a little garden next to the station – it seemed every station-master in Hungary preferred fuchsias – and there at the end of the garden, like an illustration from a German postcard, stood Rozina with a parasol in her hand. Sindbad kissed both her hands, muttering incomprehensible words of adoration, and gazed enchanted at the three freckles the village sun had planted on her face.

'So you still love me?' asked Sindbad, as though it were the most important thing on earth.

'Is it possible to forget you?' answered Rozina, taking hold of Sindbad's arm as they ambled into the village.

She couldn't have been bolder and more self-confident, thought Sindbad, than if he had been her lawful husband and had just returned from a long journey: the village poplars on the grandmother's estate nodding familiarly to him, and the sheep-dog sprawling at his feet. Apple trees in gardens glance at Rozina's white legs as she passes across the dewy lawn in bare feet. In the shade of the hammock strung from the chestnut tree a little yellow flower peeps out to observe Rozina from below. A blackbird sits in the branches trying to guess what the woman is thinking behind those half-closed eyes,

'Here we are,' said Rozina as they arrived at an old country house. A moth-eaten steward's coat hung on a branch in the garden.

'I like old houses where the dead ancestors who used to live there leave their voices behind to talk at you from the walls.'

Rozina sighed. 'It was my great-grandfather who had the house built. There are a lot of chestnut trees in the area and the mice have run wild. No one here is any good at setting mousetraps. You are so clever Sindbad, you can do anything.'

'I was quite a clever child,' Sindbad answered with a certain conceit. (Mind you, who has not been a doctor, a joiner, a cobbler, or general factotum at the behest of his beloved? All men in love are children dreaming of heroic deeds. When it comes to impressing the loved one the knocking of a nail in the wall is just as heroic an enterprise as wrestling with a bear.) Sindbad took off his coat.

'Where are the traps,' he asked, rolling up his sleeves.

'Do you think they'll do?' Rozina asked anxiously, as she brought forth the little wire and wood contraptions.

The old daughter of the revolution leant on a stout stick on the veranda and watched Sindbad through thick round glasses as he busied himself with the traps.

'An officer and gentleman,' she whispered to her grand-daughter.

The moon had risen above the distant woods and the grandmother, having thrown her stick a few times at the clumsy chambermaid, grumbled a little, sighed and went to sleep.

'Careful soldier boy doesn't run away,' she whispered in warning to Rozina.

The moon was shining through the vine leaves directly onto Rozina's face. She was as white and dreamy as an actress under a moving spotlight. Sindbad gazed in awe at her moonlit face: it was only in advanced old age that he was to discover that women are always looking into invisible mirrors. And quietly, in subdued tones full of the most noble feelings, like a faint bell tinkling above a river, he told Rozina that ever since childhood he had been seeking a face like hers. In his childhood dreams, as he turned off his desk light, this woman's face would appear radiantly before him. On all his journeys, on all his aimless wanderings, this was the face that called to him and drew him on. This was the face with whose image he was born, that had glimmered in his cradle, until the moment he made its acquaintance as an adult when he first noticed it on a balcony in Aranykéz Street.*

'Señora,' proclaimed Sindbad with absolute solemnity, 'I will never again be able to live without you.'

Rozina reciprocated the urgent squeeze of his hand. 'Speak,' she sighed gently and equally seriously. 'Your words are fluttering round my head like the miraculous singing of invisible birds.'

She inclined her head as if following the progress of the moon. Her black eyes opened to such a size one might have thought she had suddenly lost track of it. She grasped his arm urgently and complained in a sorrowful voice. 'I have no one but you ... If you were to leave me, Sindbad, I wouldn't know what to do. Speak to me. Whisper lovely soft things in my ear. It'll be as if you really loved me.'

Sindbad stared at a cloud that had swum across the moon and was convinced the words that came to him now were inscribed on those jasper-coloured sails. Love. Love.

The woman trembled, stood up suddenly and pointed into a dark corner. 'A mouse,' she hissed with repulsion.

She had turned deathly pale, her hand shook and she broke into uncontrollable sobbing. 'A mouse!' she repeated, shuddering.

Sindbad smiled a heroic smile, lit a candle and threw the first mousetrap which had served its purpose out into the yard together with its victim.

'Idiot!' cried the woman, trembling in fury. 'I won't even be able to step out into the yard. Is that what you want? I hate and despise mice.'

Sindbad smiled wearily. 'It is a very little mouse,' he muttered.

'Go. I hate the sight of you. You have killed a mouse. Murderer,' she spluttered. 'I loathe you. I don't love you. Don't you dare touch me with those hands. Be off with you.'

'It was a very small mouse,' Sindbad repeated, easily offended like most lovers, and he took his hat and cloak and waited a while before the house in case his darling called him back. The house was silent. So, with a genuine reason for sadness this time, Sindbad wandered off towards the station in time to catch the night train. Later, after he had become a ghost, he developed a particular grudge against mice.

The Unforgettable Compliment

T here is a small town in the highlands which in
Sindbad's day ('In my day,' as men who are sick
at heart tend to say) was notorious for its women,
who would spend the day unkempt, bleary-eyed, their
hair uncombed, beating their husbands and their children, screeching in loud birdlike voices, carrying sauce-
pans full of cabbage, rising at dawn to do their laundry,
competing with broad-footed Saxon girls, sticking their
heads into the cobwebs in the attic and climbing up the
flue with slippers flapping on their bare feet. Indeed,
there was only one proper lady in the town, an impoverished countess who wore old-fashioned military
kid gloves when she did her housework. But as the day
went by, once the sleeping crows and jackdaws in the
clocktower had travelled a full half revolution, once the
autumn titmouse was calling ever more softly in the
apple tree, once cellar doors were opening all around
town and the icy, tempting, casket-perfumed air poured
from the hills and blue shadows settled across the
rooftops like stories told by travellers through the forest,
as it darkened towards evening, the very same ill-kempt
women put on their finery, drew on elegant shoes, fixed
blazing jewels in their combed hair, washed their faces

as thoroughly as if preparing for a ball and wore such expressions of delight the desire for pleasure seemed to ripple across them like lamplight on water. And so they brought out sweet-scented stockings, lace collars, attractive scarves, white gloves and plumed hats ... Sometimes they just sat in the window watching the deserted street, at other times they paced along with a spring in their step as if about some business, passing through the market, by the chemist, swinging their hips past the bookseller's lit window. They would chat together about Paris and Pest, and happily link arms as the snow gently fell. A strange man is standing in the inn's draughty doorway under the lantern with its red lettering. The omnibus toddles from the Poplar Inn towards the railway station, and the one-eyed servant Tirnovai stands on the running board wearing a gilded cap. Who will the omnibus fetch from the station and who is that strange melancholy-looking gentleman standing there with his hands in his pockets? The cut of his clothes suggests he is from the capital and, the nerve of it, he is wearing a tie pin in the shape of a ballerina's leg. And why doesn't he say anything to anyone there at the end of the street where the road bends round towards the little bridge where the street lighting stops? Who can he be? What would he say if someone were to speak to him? What would he have to say about where he has come from? And if he spoke, would he pay some woman a compliment that she would not forget as long as she lived?

Sindbad, who used to spend his winters in little towns like this one, took stock of the women passing the

environs of the Poplar Inn, and always had a compliment ready which he might whisper, however indifferently, perhaps even with an air of mild boredom, into
the ears of local village women before they returned
home and changed into their dowdier indoor garments.
He knew for certain that they would hesitate in the
candlelight before the mirror and glance at themselves
approvingly before undoing the first clip. They'd look
in the mirror, smile vaguely and think of the fine words
and lies they had been told in the darkness. And as they
stood before the mirror in this fashion it might seem that
their one and only desire might be never to take those
clothes off, since it was these that made them desirable,
unforgettable objects of love. This was how they had
glittered, if only for a few minutes, under the lights of
the promenade. The tap-tap of their delicate shoes
evoked the music of Budapest – or so Sindbad persuaded them –, their jewels borrowed their fire from
those seen in the boxes of the Royal Opera House in
Vienna with the Princess Annunciata seated in the left-
hand row. As for their hair, their eyes, their mouths –
he had never seen the like. Only when he looked into
those particular eyes was he aware of the bluish tinge
of the March winds as they blew through the wood; only
'her' hair carried the delicious fragrance of lilacs such
as decorate the altar at a young girl's wedding; 'her'
mouth alone breathed the odour of summer evenings
after the watering of the gardens. As for their gait
beneath those fashionably short skirts, they reminded
Sindbad of precious moments at the Grand Opera when

the tulle-skirted quadrille advanced and Donizetti's score lay open on the conductor's music stand.

'Wouldn't it be nice to ride into town at the head of a troop of marauding janissaries,' sighed Sindbad.

'And?'

'And to ravish you away.' And mocking laughter would break from Sindbad's lips.

There were a number of autograph books in whose pages Sindbad's name might have been found, though his stays were usually short: he wouldn't wait too long under the bridge, his hands thrust into pockets, his green hat on his head, for any woman. After his resurrection he often sought out this town of passionate women; he would visit the cellars with the men and scrawl his name on the cellar walls as light-heartedly as he did in the autograph books. In theatres and restaurants he sat behind the women and promised to visit them next when their husbands were out. He spoke to their shoulders and necks and his hands never strayed into the folds of their dresses. He invited the women to die with him, or to run away over the border. And now, at twilight, when he saw them again passing the old bridge where, under snow-covered roofs, the yellow curtains of the little café were as luminous and bright as castles in the puppet theatre, that long-extinct volcano, his heart, felt something extraordinary stirring in it. He was deeply moved.

The tip-tap of those little shoes as the women drew nearer conjured ineffable hours, days of splendour which crept into his heart, swooped into it as lightly as a swallow entering its nest. He recalled passionate words, sighs and cries escaping from women's closed lips, those gestures and kisses by which they bound him. And somehow their faces appeared before him as clearly as they did at those rendezvous in the graveyard, among the beechwoods on some hillside, under a Christmas tree or on a veranda laden with winter plants. It was as if their faces had petrified – those eyes, those mouths – all that time ago, so that all their lives they could express but one emotion: love.

Sindbad stood invisible by the columns of the bridge and allowed the women to drift past him, whereas in the past he would swiftly tuck his hand under their arms or into their muffs. And how those delicate ears would redden in the flood of passionate words.

Now they passed him in the winter dusk: the goldsmith's wife, her eyes sparkling with devotion and temptation; the lady-stationer who once confessed to an old love and selflessly entertained Sindbad by entrusting him with all her secrets; the dreamy schoolmistress who spent the most blissful of afternoons warbling deliciously about theosophy and the immortality of the soul; the pianist who relented only at the moment of farewell; Irma, who delivered sleepy observations about her beautiful sister, Janka; Johanna, who fled into the neighbouring town on a sledge with the intention of killing herself; Aranka, who reminded him of her wealth and promised her lover a carefree future; Maria, who kept thinking of her Easter confessional … and Lelia, who wanted nothing from him save that he come back. The ghost on the bridge saw bygone hours pass across old familiar faces as if time had failed to give them a good scrub and wash the kisses away.

How many declarations since then – to other men, on other occasions, in other words? But this did not occur to the dead man who, like an old maid himself, could think of nothing but the compliments, the words of the women locked in his heart and never forgotten.

The last to pass over the bridge was the teacher of mathematics who was much respected in town for the calm clarity of her thought. Her face always smelled of cold water and she wore a white collar above her tight bodice. Sindbad stepped from the shadows.

'Do you remember me?'

The teacher stared at Sindbad for some time in considerable surprise. When she smiled faintly it was like dreaming on an early spring evening when late blossom covers the apple tree like a white veil.

'I do remember you,' she answered and squeezed Sindbad's hand. 'You told me I was like Dr Faustus in female form. I have often thought of the Doctor since then.'

Sentimental Journey

Sindbad heard a peculiar noise in his dream. From inside the coffin it sounded like clods of earth falling into his grave. He had been dreaming of women, as usual, of weary shoulders that had once glimmered at him, of young women's ankles, and of the fine heads of hair he had noted here and there on his travels. The peculiar knocking woke him and he raised his head from the pillow thinking he had died. A charlatan had once told him – and this had been confirmed by a fortune teller – that he would die suddenly. Death would be like a guest from a far-off land suddenly entering the gate. Or somebody walking in the opposite direction down a long path or in the busy traffic of the city, a figure you'd pick out among a thousand. Death was an evil-looking, unpleasant foreign man with piercing eyes, who had been sizing him up from a distance. They'd approach each other, getting ever closer. Sindbad's knees would go weak and only cowardice would keep him moving forwards in the hope he might be able to avoid the malevolent stranger. He'd feel dizzy, shut his eyes tight and hold his breath. Sometimes this invisible dizziness surprised him, as if someone had thrown a butterfly net over his head and this weighed so heavy on his skull and his eyes that he would forget everything that had ever happened to him. He clutched at wayside trees and felt he was on a funicular into the other world with strange indifferent faces around him. It was as if he had suddenly become invisible: women who yesterday would have looked him in the eye and allowed the flame of his desire to leap in the depths of their own, now hid their mouths and lips when Sindbad cast a bold glance at them; men with vacant looks whom Sindbad would ordinarily have ignored and held in contempt, since he had listened to so many of them, learned their ways, knew their sad passions, their demeaning lusts, their unforgivable blunderings in love; all these passed him by with expressions of utter indifference while he clung to a lamp-post, numb and dazed, like a fish drowning in air. Whole minutes would pass as he employed all his strength and energy to free himself of the gripping vortex of death and return to reality; it was like the raising of a grey veil, its colours like those you might find on the sides of a disinterred coffin. He took a deep breath: that is how I shall die, he thought, and had taken at least a dozen steps before he noticed a pair of forget-me-not blue eyes shining under a straw hat prinked out with flowers. 'It was a minor stroke,' he said later to himself, aloud, as if jeering at a retreating enemy. He walked down the avenue of poplars and there was no malevolent-looking antagonist striding towards him, only some shy, dark-haired and as yet innocent, women ambling along in a perfectly friendly manner.

'I'm sure I hadn't been thinking of anyone in particular then, that afternoon,' Sindbad reflected at the opera one evening, the conductor having announced the interval. He thought of death as a cudgel blow which might perhaps strike him as he lay in the arms of his beloved. At least it would have the decency to intervene by a lakeside or some deep river where he might disappear almost immediately. And sitting alone in his room at midnight, his favourite book of verses or some sad old romance having dropped from his hands, it occurred to him how awkward it would be if certain women were to meet at his funeral. Though most of them would probably only watch from a distance, as if they had nothing to do with him. Only one or two naïve ones, of the sort he had cheated, would blub their eyes out at the graveside, and he hadn't much cared for them anyway. But he wasn't dead yet, though he could still hear that odd coffin-like rattling even after having had a good look around the room and recognised all the furniture. On the wall there was a photograph of a young girl lying dead on her bier, her half-closed eyes peering with otherworldly calm out of the small circular gilt frame. Here a lady of Queen Elizabeth's time stands stiff-waisted in smoky oil colours, the notes of an imagined Hungarian folk song fluttering around her brown hair. Wrapped in her own thoughts a female fairy glances down from the wall: Sindbad has never met her but has always believed she would visit his room some time and, finding him absent, draw off her gloves, extend her arm from beneath her sable fur and write a few lines in blue ink sprinkled with gold powder on a very white sheet of paper to say she had called and was inexpressibly grieved not to have met him. There is no man living who does not believe that one day she will simply turn up, that most precious, most tender of women, whom he has known only in his imagination, someone he has dreamed of since he was a child and has failed to meet only because she happened to be a dancer in Seville or a Tartar princess in the Caucasus. Or perhaps she has long ago turned into an old lady who is astonished to find that her tarot shows a knight-in-arms destined especially for her, and however superstitiously she shuffles and lays out the deck the result is the same; or, conversely, she is still running about the playground in a little skirt while her nanny is dreaming romantic dreams about the poet Kisfaludy, or she is someone glimpsed at the window of a galloping coach, or a stranger arriving in town in the dawn hours, seen climbing the stairs of a sleepy house with a newspaper in her hand. Who knows where she is to be found, that woman in the music of whose voice one might hear the mingled chimes of life and death? And nobody ever steps out of that dream into reality. But what would be the point of dreaming if dreams came true?

It was spring and Sindbad was leaning nonchalantly on the parapet of the bridge, gazing at the fast-flowing river, his mind like a conscientious schoolboy's, dreaming of the towns, villages and hamlets that the white foam would pass through after it had vanished from his sight. He imagined scenes in humid sunlit mist or by the light of shepherds' campfires; he saw fishermen pulling at oars while a solitary girl wandered the shore, gathering courage, clutching her child to her heart; he saw men with wild bloodshot eyes sinking into the waves and a

little village further downstream where the body of
some fine fellow slides to rest on the grassy bank, while
that very evening the heavy hulk of the steam packet
bound for the south cuts through the waves to the
accompaniment of a guitar and a ringing baritone voice.
There on the shore lies the drowned victim, his frenzied
eyes staring at the stars, stars contemplated by a legion
of other eyes. That unseeing glance may be telling the
Dog Star or the Great Bear about the woman who is even
now strolling on the deck with her new admirer's arm
about her waist, and they too may be searching for some
star that will guard their steps, to whom they may sigh
as they gaze out of their window late at night, in whose
name they might exchange their vows. And the women,
swimming beside the men in the same current, deep
beneath the waves or rising to the surface, as they pass
the towns they used to know, where once they were
happy to dawdle in the café, remember the strange
words that passed behind vanilla-coloured curtains,
words of their own, words they hadn't thought to hear
from a woman's mouth, or of the promenade where a
man confessed that the most unfortunate thing he had
ever done was to come to this town, and how the future
appeared to offer him nothing but a prospect of endless
misery. Now they were all swimming together, silent as
the fish that nuzzled at their eyes and their hearts as if
wanting to know where they had come from, what they
had seen before they had fled contact with human eyes
and escaped into these dark corridors of water? Gloat-
ing, wicked, sly and soulless eyes – that's the reason
anyone leaves town, after all. Under the island, at the

bend of the river, where calm waves that seem to know where they are going eddy and whirl in confusion, male and female corpses meet and touch in the murmuring tide, and should they be washed to shore together, with what peculiar expressions they examine each other! No one here bothers to ask the question 'Why?' Perhaps they are no longer thinking of what happened yesterday – what the pillow told them, what words were spoken by mouths or what eyes had lied to them! Here on the shore, they sprawl on the grass until peasants find them and go through their pockets, keeping silence like old friends. That woman might have been on the till somewhere in the Josephstown district. She might have leapt into the flood on account of a soldier, so that she could follow him in some way to his border post at Zimony. The man might be weeping for his darling, now conveying her innermost thoughts by means of kisses into the mouth of another, having not even bothered to turn up for one last meeting at the lease-room hotel where he had been waiting for her with a loaded revolver. What peculiar glances might they be casting at each other now in the passing stream?

Having heard the rattling of the coffin, Sindbad, our hero, was lost in contemplation of his lover who yesterday had leapt into the Danube.

'I shall wear my blue veil,' her farewell letter said, among many other things.

Sindbad silently thought that he would do nothing to avoid his own approaching death. And what had she been up to in the meanwhile, there in the River Danube, since he last saw her? What sights had she seen, what had she heard since they had shared their pillow talk the night before? She might have all kinds of sweet witty things to say that he might listen to drowsily. What splendid stories women might tell once their appetite for love had passed?

Sindbad looked round. He was quite alone on the bridge. Slowly he let himself down into the Danube to meet his dead darling somewhere under the island.

And perhaps he met a number of other female suicides on his way.

The Children's Eyes

In the course of his various deaths – like an invisible passenger beside the driver of a mail coach to whom the women of the neighbourhood blow kisses and wave farewell as the coach sets off from some inn at the end of town, and the horn is blowing, and insomniacs peer from behind their curtains, and the wheels clatter all night down uneven roads that seem to have been built over empty wine cellars into unfamiliar towns – Sindbad revisited all the places where he had ever been particularly happy or unhappy. Fate willed that he should travel as a ghost until the great day of salvation chose to arrive. For some months he took shelter in an empty crypt under the threshold of a highland church whose occupant had wandered off somewhere. All day he watched legs stepping over the stones and learned to recognise people by them. Already there were a few well-known old acquaintances whose tap-tap he could tell from some way off, and he kissed the heels of beautiful women as they passed over him, sighing so violently that the flat stone above the crypt seemed to move. (The women in question would snatch their skirts together and, having occupied their place on the pew, would pick up the prayer book that had been lying there since their grandmothers' time and leaf through for a prayer against the temptations of the devil.) Brides, hesitantly treading girls in white silk slippers and virginal stockings, dressed head to foot in fresh new clothes, and sweet little blouses whose monograms had not yet been closely inspected by any man – Sindbad would have married them all if he could, if only he was able to get out from beneath the church steps. His attentive gaze followed the women as they went in to pray and whenever he saw tears in their eyes this had such a violent effect on him he was practically out of his skin with concern. This state of affairs continued until one day the proper inhabitant of the crypt returned from his wanderings and demanded his place back.

'Allow me to expiate my crimes in peace, sir. My corpse has been trampled over by all kinds of beggars and whores.'

So Sindbad got back on the mail coach again and tried to tell from approaching inn signs whether the town ahead was familiar or not. (The innkeepers' wives had grown uncommonly old in these parts: ah, how he had lied to them, whispering in their ears how together they could lure some rich traveller into the house, then rob him, or manufacture counterfeit coins in the cellar, coins of such quality no one could tell them from the original; how he had promised he'd abandon his vagabond life, take the business in hand and within a few years make such a success of it they would be in a position to buy that aristocratic villa that had been on the market some time!) One evening the mail coach drove through the outskirts of a town and passed an inn bearing the arms of the 'Star of St Leopold', whose fine name, roast suckling pig and particularly delicious herring salad had remained a fond memory of Sindbad's over several years.

'There used to be two sisters in this town, both of whom were deeply in love with me,' he thought to himself and unceremoniously took leave of his friend, the side-whiskered driver.

The moon was standing directly above the many-storeyed tower of the church where he stopped to question a vagrant ghost about parish affairs. The spirit answered everything politely and precisely until Sindbad broached the subject of local women, at which point it broke into the most vile oaths. 'Do not mention those women in my presence,' raged the ghost as the tower-warden's wife tipped a bucket of water over them for disturbing the silence.

Sindbad later discovered that the furious ghost was called Charlie by the women. He had been a weaver and his speciality used to be to stand by his loom and sing hymns in order that the cloth should attain a particular whiteness and brightness, while the women called to him through the window, 'Charlie, Charlie dear!' The upshot of all this was that he went and hanged himself.

Just before the cock crew Sindbad met a tipsy musician who had spent the whole night entertaining the spirits of drunken revolutionaries in a ruined cellar and was on his way back to the graveyard. From him he discovered that the ladies who once loved him now lived in the market square and had married rich elderly middle-class gentlemen; that even now it was their sport to steal each other's lovers, admirers and benefactors and that only recently one sister had tried to poison the other.

'I like the sound of this town. How nice to find myself here at last,' Sindbad murmured under his breath and let the musician go on his way. A violin passed him on invisible legs. When they buried the musician they had propped the violin next to his coffin.

One of the women was called Mitzi, the other Eugenia. (Eugenia was particularly insistent that gentlemen should pronounce every letter of her name, and preferably with a slight sing-song pursing of the lips – Mitzi, after all, was just a common shop-girl's kind of name.) So, after the daylight hours which he spent in the cemetery dicing with dead mercenary soldiers, occasionally laughing out loud to himself, as soon as it grew dark, Sindbad set out to find the women. It was Eugenia who had made him swear to forsake all forms of gambling, from cards through to the roulette table, as she rifled her father's safe for old gold ornaments from whose shining surfaces kings in full-bottomed wigs and ancient queens with lily-white necks glanced anxiously at Sindbad galloping off to the smoky French Room of the 'Star of St Leopold', where a fat barber and a cardsharp in a white waistcoat dealt the deck for a round of faro.

It was spring in the town then and it was as if Sindbad had brought his gospel of flowery phrases, instant promises and complex lies expressly to these naïve, pure-hearted young women. (Soon enough autumn would arrive with all its sadness, its huddlings by barely burning fires, its rain streaming down the windows like women's tears, a time for consoling abandoned ladies and reading appropriate passages from books of verse, for sitting together, listening to the strange sounds of the wind.) Eugenia was in the big room with a wealthy admirer whom she dismissed, saying, 'I need to discuss the rent with Mr Sindbad.' Moneybags, a red-eyed, unmannerly man with an over-confident belly and rather tight-fitting clothes, took full stock of Sindbad while waiting for his hat. 'I'll give you a sound thrashing for that,' thought the traveller who had been known to brawl with tough coach-drivers at the Blue Cat in his youth.

'Sindbad!' cried Eugenia, as if she had only become aware of his presence after her admirer's departure. 'Where on earth have you been? What delightful places have you travelled to? Have you had many lovers? Have you returned with the gorgeous flame of youth when you loved only me?'

The traveller ran his eye over the lady, taking in every detail. Her nose seemed to have grown a little since the days he used to watch tiny white clouds break across her narrow forehead while making love to her. It had not been quite straight even then. Her eyes now dissimulated those emotions which had once been genuine: devotion, humility and entreaty. Her nostrils seemed blacker now that she applied copious amounts of rice-powder to her face. And what had happened to that innocent mouth with its unselfconscious smile which used to look as if some wandering apostle who had spent the night on her floor had taken his leave by kissing her lightly on those childish lips while she was sleeping?

That saintly man would have travelled on wrapped in his blue cloak until he found his final resting place on the church wall of some pious village, but the smile would have remained on the virgin's mouth right through dawn into the day – a smile for whose sake Sindbad was once prepared to rob and even murder. Ah, but nowadays that twitching of the mouth, the occasional moistening of those extraordinary deceivers, the corners of the lips, the treacherous sparkling of the eyes, just like children playing with a signalling mirror on a fine summer afternoon, the self-conscious arching of the neck and the curious rolling of the letter 'r' – these were part of the repertoire of any lady who knows perfectly well that in a sunlit corner of a small garden, there where the shadows begin, the light material of her dress becomes transparent and that men are so infinitely stupid that one blazing ring on a white hand or a pink garter tied with a heart-shaped May Day favour or the sudden raising of an eye, until then firmly fixed on the ground, accompanied by a slightly whorish movement of the arms is enough to occupy them in their loneliness.

'There has been a lot of lying here before me,' thought Sindbad.

'And of all your lovely plans, which have come to fruition, my dear friend?' spoke the woman and moved her legs as if to draw attention to her green stockings. 'Your brothers and sisters – what became of them? Your little sister of whom you used to speak with such tenderness? Your sweet old mother, who I wanted to meet, so that I might kneel before her, kiss her hand and ask her for her blessing?'

Sindbad calmly let his eyes rest on her silk dress. He nodded without taking up any of these matters.

'Ah, this town is so boring – you can't imagine how boring it is, Sindbad,' the woman continued. 'Every day the same people, the compliments of the chemist, the jokes of the vet! ... The blazing eyes of the young men at Sunday Mass and when they stop going to church they never even notice me. Oh, ageing is terrible for women who were once surrounded by eager admirers who followed them everywhere with their eyes, the whole town apparently populated by wandering actors, a thousand Romeos, my dear sir – and then to find those glances cooling, and even the captain of the fire brigade only comes to dinner when I cook him his favourite meal.'

Sindbad nodded sadly.

'It's just not good enough!' cried Eugenia in a sudden fury, then cast her eyes down and smiled. 'At least you should see my children.'

In a few minutes three little girls stood before Sindbad. Their hair was cut straight – they looked like three pretty little lapdogs. Their mother rewarded them with a sweet each.

'Heavens, if only I had children,' sighed Sindbad plaintively, 'I'd be forever carrying them on my shoulders, playing with them in the garden and mending their shirts ... I'd stare into their pretty little souls like a dreamy traveller gazing into a mountain tarn. I would talk only to them because I would hate to waste my words on anyone else.'

'They are pretty, aren't they?' muttered Eugenia, lost in thought. 'But I would like to see you again, Sindbad. When I'm alone I often start crying and I don't even know why. Perhaps I'm weeping for you. I want to see you. So that you can talk to me about my children, since up till now people have only complimented me on my legs and these poor feet squeezed into these tiny shoes. I let the shoes hurt so that wandering actors should find me attractive. Oh, I'm so ashamed of myself.'

'The children's eyes might bring me this way again,' the traveller answered quietly.

Mine

———

Mitzi was a childless woman and would look
away distractedly when the ladies of the town
started talking of their children and discussing
their thousand upon thousand accomplishments and
particularities in her presence. For mothers, sons are an
inflated embodiment of characteristics they used to
dream of, dwell on and guess at in men, and daughters
are repositories of those beauties and talents they had
once hoped to discover in themselves. In provincial
towns, where the fashion magazines are delivered once
a fortnight, where wandering actresses do not dance
nightly at the sign of the Linden and where seducers are
eventually known for what they are, children assume an
overwhelming importance in women's lives. Women
behave well, give birth often and it is not unusual for
them to blossom suddenly at fifty, to find their second
spring when late buds appear on the apple tree they
thought only fit for firewood in the domestic hearth.
Once more they stroll arm in arm with their husbands
with an air of happy abandon, and tip their heads
dreamily to one side as they did when they were brides
and maids. So Mitzi, who was highly conscious of her
position as leading lady of this town where stone effi-

gies of stern-eyed bearded men gazed down from the church walls while women went to confession, would have been glad to discover at her knee one day a child or two whom she could dress in white stockings and little sailor suits. When she was alone – providing no one could see her daydreaming, lost in a serious trance, watching and blowing away the smoke of her slim cigarette as the French novel slid from her hand – she could see a little ragamuffin dressed in a shirt, standing in the corner, waving a thick-handled riding crop. Mitzi stretched her hand out to the child but there was only a rocking horse by the wall. A young merchant had brought it to her once, having purchased it at some market on the shores of the distant Volga. The tail of the horse formed a flute that could actually be played. On these occasions Mitzi would give a loud sigh and rub the illusion from her eyes. (Mitzi's husband, Matthew, was a hollow old beech-tree, who only felt happy when he was in a wood. He was a wood merchant come rain or shine and was more interested in what lay under a tree's bark than in his wife's dreams. 'I must buy her a ruby ring,' he thought whenever he remembered her in the course of his travels.)

This was the broad picture Sindbad obtained of Mitzi's life after consultation with a drunken old Pole who used to walk up and down the town in his choir-master's velvet coat, entertaining his students with wicked gossip, regaling them with embellished versions of local love affairs. That is until the brandy in him finally caught fire and burned him out, which event was greeted with a hearty 'Thank Heaven!' from the young (but also mature) women, into whose hands the choir-master-cum-knight errant had smuggled notes from young landowners, traders fresh from market, or indeed from anyone prepared to cross his own palm with coin of a certain reassuring weight.

Ever since then he was to be found sitting at the cemetery gates dangling his stockinged and slippered feet and grinning ironically at the little town spread out along the hillside. 'And who was your sweetheart? Who did you love, sir? Whose favours did you enjoy?' the ghost asked Sindbad when the latter turned up on pretence of humbly requesting that he should be allowed to sing a motet or two in his spare time. Old brandy-breath looked him up and down. 'I see from your appearance you are neither a travelling merchant nor a bored hunter fresh from court, so why should I lie to you? This wounded little pigeon arranged her affairs so cleverly I could never quite keep track of her – though, as you know sir, I can't vouch for everyone. A half-crazy flautist hung around town for a while making a nuisance of himself, until I eventually drove him out. He had a collection of old sheet music out of which he compiled a romance that he dedicated to Madam Mitzi.'

In other words Sindbad knew practically nothing of his old love, one of the two sisters who had adopted him the last time he was in town. He attended on them and they sewed him a Polish-style felt coat to keep him warm in winter, lining it with the black lambswool they had borrowed from their father's fur travelling outfit. He slipped past the pretty chambermaid who walked across the snow-white rugs covering the floor in bare feet, as was the custom. Naturally, he couldn't help touching her as he went and she cursed the apparently over-familiar black cat nearby who, she assumed, had rubbed himself against her.

The woman was leaning on the windowsill, half kneeling on a well-padded chair, and as she was wearing only a light nightdress, Sindbad could take proper stock of her figure. She seemed quite slender in the waist – 'even as a girl she used to order girdles from Vienna,' he remembered – yet there was something plump about her, as there is about many bored women who from quite early in the afternoon like to nibble chocolates or preserved fruit while lolling on the bed, promising themselves that the next day they really will go out and weed the garden, but who somehow always end up munching an apple; they bring ice-cream home in cool, green-painted tin dishes, and later in the evening, once guests are no longer expected, they like to gnaw at a stick of garlic-flavoured dry wurst … Her white stocking had a very pleasant scent, the frill at the hem of her skirt was sparkling white, and the bow on her slipper was like the ribbon in the hair of some cheerful convent girl. Her gown was embroidered with a pattern of oriental flowers in honour of the long silent musical clock that no longer amused her with Mozart's 'Rondo alla turca' but which might just spring to life, just as the ringlets on her neck might go some way to conjuring up the merry month of May with its scented grasses growing on dewy white hillsides. Her ear lobes were as translucent as the marble out of which the figure of Venus had been carved, her breasts the kind that novice monks must dream of. There was the palest of shadows above her upper lip, a down of youth such as you see on young boys wrestling in the grass. Her brow bore the habitual wistfulness of women deserted by their lovers.

'Maria,' cried Sindbad, moved by the sight of her, and he seized her in his arms, just as he used to do when he was a student set on conquest at all costs.

Mitzi stiffened and coiled like steel. With a single movement she sprang from Sindbad's embrace. 'I knew only you could be so presumptuous,' she responded coldly. 'I heard you had been seen about town, and would have been extremely surprised if you hadn't called. Has Eugenia invited you for supper tonight? What an easy life she has, her husband home and her children persuaded to stand guard at her side. Sadly I am always alone, my husband is always buying and selling tracts of woodland. I am amazed I didn't hear your footsteps, particularly as I happened to be thinking of you.'

'I have been dead for years,' Sindbad answered, 'and the door only opens before me if someone urgently desires me to call. You called, so here I am. My dear, my sweet Maria. What do you want to tell me?'

With a movement that might have been interpreted as flirtatious, but could equally have been simply clumsy, Mitzi offered Sindbad a chair, as she did to the red-moustached council officer who tended to call when her husband was away. 'Sit down, dear friend, you who were the foolishness of my youth, my sin, my amusement. Who is wearing the coat lined with black lamb's wool now? Do the girls still go to Mass on an early

December morning, while their darling kneels thought-fully beside the altar in his red skirts and ceremoniously rings the bell? Eugenia and I stood in the choir and the tears flowed from our eyes. Rooks were whirling in the fog above the rooftops, the villagers were coming and going in the market like ghosts and always it was your scarlet skirts we saw. Do you still love me as you did then, when your prayers were addressed to me?'

'If I were alive I would kiss your foot now in precisely the same mad devoted fashion,' answered Sindbad.

'It is because you are long dead that I dare speak of you like this, Sindbad. I want a child. A strong, dark-haired boy with a fine large head. A little bear cub I could no longer manage once he turned five years old – who would hang the cat with a length of string and set fire to my bed. A bad, spiteful little boy, that's what I want, one I could tame and educate as I once did you when you wanted to break the door open at night, and stabbed my arm with a knife, who, when I knelt on the floor, bit my ankle. That's the kind of boy I want.'

The woman bent her head as if at the confessional, a penitent trying to recall whether there was anything else she should reveal to God's anointed. She seized Sind-bad's hand. 'One that is mine, mine alone!'

The Woman Who Told Tales

———————

This story concerns Mrs Boldogfalvi, a high-living lady of years gone by, who excelled both at prayer and at lying to men. Many years had passed since the first happy lie which slipped from her lips in the florists in Servita Square as she was tucking a fresh spring buttonhole into the lapel of an elderly earl. French authors have long ago described the process whereby little flower girls become great ladies, a process which begins with arranging violets in the shadow of some ancient church and reading small advertisements in the daily press, distinguishing one male customer from another only by the scent of a waxed moustache. These moustaches always appeared at a proud height above the little flower girl's head. A small trick of the eyes and the mouth and these proud male embellishments were enticed closer (at least such used to be the way poor women could devastate a man's heart).

Mrs Boldogfalvi's magnificent lies, her startling good looks, and her modest accommodating manner, which seemed to approve everything men said to her, however idiotic, allowed the good creature to spend her life without too many cares, now delicately sparkling, other times withdrawing into silence, like a precious stone hidden in a deep wooden chest. She knew many men and succeeded in finding favour with every one of them. Those signs of weakness, vanity and all too frequent stupidity that a wise woman may detect in any man, she cultivated with an extraordinary selfless devotion. True that Mrs Boldogfalvi depended on ever more elaborate lies in order to hold the attention of her male acquaintances. By now she had consumed an entire library of novels and committed to memory countless fine phrases, figures of speech and apt comparisons culled from the works of passionate poets. And by the time the years really began to weigh heavily on her, Mrs Boldogfalvi was so caught up both in the life of the metropolis and of the country that she was eminently capable of entertaining guests without recourse to novels altogether.

She succeeded in cultivating the perfectly appropriate lie, the lie that each particular ear was most pleased to hear. As every man seemed to demand his own specific legend or myth so Mrs Boldogfalvi kept a vast store of them. There was one for the earl, one for the student, one for the impoverished poet, and she told each his own, quietly, quaintly and with utter conviction, so that the listener began to recognise the circumstances and lineaments of his own life within it. This subtle woman could even gain access to the deepest recesses of the soul, those depths you reach only when you can't sleep. Is it not the case that everyone would soonest hear the story he believes in his heart of hearts, the one where he dreams his own life? Mrs Boldogfalvi would fix her listener with sad eyes full of childlike sincerity. 'Oh it's not your life I'm talking about, I've no means of knowing that. I'm talking about someone else, a stranger. Interesting though, isn't it?'

Sindbad, who spent part of his early life at the feet of the said lady listening with amazement to her lies, wondered at men's credulity, nobility and good nature when, without a moment's thought, they drained the brew that Mrs Boldogfalvi had carefully prepared for them. After his death Sindbad would visit the place where once – near the walls of an old church during Eastertide services, when the pious tillers of the soil waited with bowed heads for the priest to bless their fodder – he leaned against the wall, reading poems from a little book, half listening to the boom of the organ and the reedy voice of the rector at his psalms. Sindbad never even noticed the woman riding in his direction, until her horse reared above him like a performing pony before a circus ringmaster. It took some effort on the woman's part to bring the horse under control. And as she patted its neck with her gloved hands her lively long-lashed eyes looked deep into his: it was as if she had sprung straight from a novel by Miklós Jósika.

('You had a remarkably interesting face,' Mrs Boldogfalvi told him later, once Sindbad had settled on his cushion to hear the nonsense calculated to drive good sense out of him. 'I was curious about you, about your green cloak and about the book of poetry, and there was a strange point of light swimming in your eyes, like a lamp seen through net curtains, something that always attracted me to a man.')

At that time Mrs Boldogfalvi was being pursued by a particularly jealous lover and used to be escorted around the country by officers of the hussars. (Her husband was not much interested in her travels, preferring the husbandry of bees. He read newspapers a year after they appeared once they had worked their way through to the top of the beehive and had turned a deep yellow.) The jealous young man had made a few foolish threats and would sit in the corner nursing the darkest of thoughts without ever once taking his menacing eyes off her. So she was on the run, not by coach, since the carriage wheels would leave deep marks on the ground, but on horseback, a horse's hooves being harder to trace. The young man needed time to forget, to find peace or, failing that, to commit suicide. This was how Mrs Boldogfalvi happened to find herself in the uplands, by the wall of that particular church at that particular Eastertide, just when Sindbad happened to be leaning against it.

They ordered dinner at the sign of The Bear where Sindbad had his lodgings. Sunset found him sitting by the window, dreaming of distant landscapes when there was a soft knock at the door, and before he could answer, in stepped Mrs Boldogfalvi.

'Pardon me, sir. I am a stranger in the town and you seem like a gentleman.'

Sindbad stared in surprise at the lady before him in her little black riding costume and her Queen Elizabeth hat as she settled unconcernedly onto the arm of the worn old settee and tapped the ground with her little spurs as she spoke.

'I will be travelling on with my escort, some cheerful young officers who provide me with good company. They're not likely to start duelling with each other. Not one of them regards the other as dispensable. I can't stand jealous men.'

Sindbad smiled. He felt he had known this woman a long long time ago. Her voice went straight to his heart. It was as if they had been engaged in conversation for years before this meeting.

'Mind you, you look like a man who could be jealous,' said Mrs Boldogfalvi, tapping her riding boots with her jasper-studded crop.

'I admit it,' Sindbad muttered. 'I have expected the women I loved to be faithful. I cannot share with others. All their thoughts, their every word, had to be mine alone. Even their dreams.'

'How sweet,' laughed the woman. 'All this is very appealing, of course, but only as long as love lasts. Looking at you I imagine you are the sort of man who quietly takes his hat, gloves and walking stick as soon as he notices he is surplus to requirements. What stupidity it is to burden a woman with your presence. How devastatingly boring it is, worse than being ill on a dull autumn afternoon, to have a man go on about his love when nobody is interested any more. I am sure you have kissed hands and bowed farewell more than once in your life, and then remembered the time spent together with gratitude. You might even have gone to say Mass at the local church and prayed for the salvation of the lady's soul. Perhaps – if you are as generous as I like to think you might be – you might even have been careful to

ensure that your faithless lover should not fall into hands
less worthy than yours, that your successor should at
least deserve the tender mercies now accorded to him.
Yes, I am sure you went when it was time to go, just
went and no longer made a nuisance of yourself.'

Sindbad contemplated this a while. 'I think I have
always departed in good time. I have never pressed my
company on a woman who was clearly trying to stifle
her yawns.'

'You see, I have not been disappointed in you. This
evening, once I have gone,' Mrs Boldogfalvi went on
in a meditative, sing-song voice, 'a blue-eyed, restless-
looking young man will come galloping into the courtyard of this inn. He will enquire about me. And if his
horse can stand the pace he will continue his pursuit of
me. I want to ask you a favour. I would like you to keep
this unhappy young man company, be kind and friendly
to him, don't let him alone. Sit with him at supper and
talk to him gently about the beauty of the end of love,
and about life, which we must strive to live through with
extraordinary grace so that we may deserve a graceful
death. You will be sure to tell the suffering blue-eyed
boy that true love can never end in scandal or in tragedy.
As the poor woman has already given him everything
let her at least keep her honour. Courtly love passes as
quietly as the distant sobbing you hear at the far end of
the wood ... And the past is not worth regretting, since
happy precious memories remain. No one can steal
those, either from him or from me. I trust, my dear
unknown friend, that you will go a little out of your way
to take care of the stranger, and if he hangs his head you

might stroke his hair, should the mood take you. Tell him that the most beautiful love affairs are those which entertain the imagination once the affair is over. The traveller is called Albert, and when he mentions a woman called Polly, be so good as to remember me, dear sir.'

Sindbad did not hesitate to agree to undertake this peculiar task.

By way of goodbye the woman took Sindbad's hand and gazed deep into his eyes. 'I want you to be a good friend to my poor, suffering boy. If ever you find yourself in Pest you are welcome to seek me out.'

She took from her glove the calling card she had prepared for him. Pauline von Boldogfalva, it said. The little spurs were already jangling down the stone steps of The Bear by the time Sindbad raised his eyes. The hussars were leaping into their saddles and galloped off after Mrs Boldogfalvi. At the church Polly turned round and looked back at the old inn, certain that Sindbad would be at the window. Then the mounted company vanished.

Sindbad stored the calling card in his wallet and walked up and down in front of The Bear. The ancient church was casting long shadows across the market-place and the bell-ringer was entering the belfry with a lit lantern in his hand.

There was a sound of galloping hooves from the south. A young man in tall riding boots, a romantic cloak and plumed hat pulled his pale horse up in front of the inn.

'The fool has arrived,' thought Sindbad. 'How strange, how amusing people are.'

The young man's face was covered in dust from his long ride, but his blue eyes shone like china. He leapt off his horse and asked after the lady rider, as she said he would. When the innkeeper told him that she had gone he cried, 'Devil take her! What am I doing wearing this fancy dress?' He glared contemptuously at his outfit and threw his plumed hat on the dining room floor. He ate voraciously, forgetting to admire the deep red of the wine set before him. He darted an impatient glance at Sindbad.

He was about thirty years of age, blond, with a milky complexion, a man brought up by women. His mother would have done his washing for him. On Sundays he would go to church just as he did when he was a little boy and sit patiently at his mother's side while the sermon droned on. He was the sort of man who would be astonished to find that not every woman had such delicate feelings as his mother, or that they had any thought but to sew on his buttons when the thread broke.

Sindbad stepped over to him and introduced himself as though they were a pair of knights errant in ancient Castile meeting at a wayside inn. In a few words he let him know that he was aware of the sorrow which drove him, Albert of the blue eyes, across the hills. Indeed, it was his good fortune to have met the deity in question.

'So you know her,' cried Albert. 'All the better that you should know the woman who insisted I dress in this courtly garb, that I wear a beret because that's the only thing she liked me in. It is for her sake I am galloping up and down the highway in this ridiculous cloak. What will a man not do for love! We all cut such pathetic figures. If Polly had demanded that I should walk the streets tarred and feathered, I would have done it for her sake!'

Sindbad gripped his new friend's hand in solidarity.

'I swear to God,' cried Albert, 'the only reason I want to see her again is to cast a contemptuous glance at her, to turn my back and ... to reject her! Yes, to reject her!'

Sindbad nodded quietly. 'We will talk about that.'

Albert Finds New Employment

That evening at The Bear, as dusk drew on and the light slowly faded in the vaulted dining room, the young knight errant was to be found with his head leaning on Sindbad's shoulder, articulately if a little shamefacedly – and not before swearing Sindbad to secrecy – telling his new friend all he knew of Mrs Boldogfalvi. It is a rare woman that all her male acquaintance describe in similar terms. Different men see the same woman in a variety of ways. One may only remember the birthmark on one side of her body, another might be able to guess what the object of desire is thinking in the evening as she goes to bed. If these various men were once to sit down together – in great old age, of course, with a few glasses to loosen their tongues – these men who had loved the same woman, granted this were possible, and they were honestly to tell each other everything they knew for certain about her, it would soon be evident that they were all speaking of a different woman. Mrs Boldogfalvi lived in at least fifty forms in men's imaginations since that was the number of men who had loved her, until, that is, they grew acquainted with death and solemnly closed their eyes for the last time. If this gathering of greybeards were to sit round a stone table, much like Heine's gathering of retired hangmen, and hold council one mysterious night, they could at best only establish certain words, certain well-defined movements where the experiences of lovers X and Y seemed to correspond. For example, when Mrs Boldogfalvi was really passionately in love she would address her lover as Milord at the most intimate moments. Milord was sometimes blond and sometimes dark. But no matter how ancient the men were they never betrayed to one another Mrs Boldogfalvi's characteristic habits. And so the majority of them, poor trusting males, believed that it was they the woman had first favoured with this loving epithet. The truth was that there were a great many Milords walking the streets of Hungary.

Albert related the story of his life to Sindbad at great length, a life which consisted chiefly of his love for Mrs Boldogfalvi. He could remember by heart the letters they had written to each other and, as you'd expect, recollect all the significant dates and days. He imputed extraordinary importance to the fact that come the evening Mrs Boldogfalvi would wait at the window of some regional manor house for him and would extend her hand for a kiss – as if she had never stood at a window before! They were very frightened of Mr Boldogfalvi and Polly often warned Albert that her husband would not hesitate to use his revolver if he ever suspected something.

Sindbad clapped his new friend on the shoulder. 'My dear friend, I myself have often heard such stories from women's lips. Indeed, they must love you a great deal if the various Messrs Boldogfalvi are prepared to shoot you. But this is only an example of false desire. Something that happens in novels.'

'Ah, dear sir, I'm only young and have little experience of life,' sighed Albert. 'To tell you the truth, this was the first lady I had ever fallen mortally in love with. She said the same about me, what is more she swore I was the first ...'

'They sincerely believe it every time they say it,' Sindbad murmured.

'And it is your opinion that Polly has addressed other men as Milord since then?'

'It is quite certain,' answered Sindbad. 'The magical power of women in Pest, and in Hungary at large, could only be broken if the oldest of men, those whom the medical profession had finally abandoned, formed a supreme tribunal to which every man worth his salt had to make a precise and honest statement about all his love affairs and every specific circumstance associated with them. Here they would recount the tricks and devices employed by certain women to draw them into their nets. They would report the words used when the women lied or told the truth on the first, second and subsequent meetings. So men would expose women before this supreme tribunal: their natural history would slowly become known and the town would no longer be haunted by mysterious, secretive demons who torture stupid and inexperienced men to distraction. Should a man observe in himself a certain interest in a lady or discover that night after night, in the street or in his dreams, he can think of nothing but that woman's name, he would apply to the tribunal and confess his desire. Then the old jurors would put their heads together and consult their records of other men's confessions and advise the troubled youth appropriately. Those old confessions would serve as useful reference points. In any case, it would help to uncover the secret of women's success more thoroughly than is usually done nowadays when every man is a potential victim. Until men are honest with each other they will never succeed in breaking the power of women.'

Albert listened carefully to what his friend told him then sighed deeply. 'So, Mr Sindbad, you really think that in the heat of passion, Polly might have addressed other men as Milord?'

'Why the devil not? A village girl turned *grande dame* would have learned such words somewhere along the line. For example, yesterday afternoon she addressed me as "dear sir",' smiled the great voyager.

'You swine!' cried Albert and leapt to his feet ready to assault Sindbad.

The voyager tenderly gestured for him to calm down.

'It's not worth it, my boy. On my word of honour, it is not worth it.'

The provincial young man sat for a long time after this, his lips twisted with pain and his eyes so full of fury that Sindbad decided there and then that should he ever find himself on a mountain top or at the edge of a cliff with only Albert as his companion, he would take great care not to be on the wrong side.

Later fury turned to tears. Albert rested his head on the table and sobbed like a child. 'All those afternoons when she knelt before me, the miserable creature, and told me the most wonderful stories! She told me her whole life story – omitting only the fact that she had cheated me in the past and was cheating me in the present. Didn't I ask her a hundred times to tell me who she had loved before she met me? Confess, my angel, after all it's over and done with. Whose head did you cradle in your arms, in whose ears did you whisper these same beautiful words? What other lovers have you regaled with stories of your childhood, your girlfriends and your acquaintances in these hours of pleasure? Who did you talk politics with? To whom did you confess your dreams or unburden your heart when you were depressed? With whom did you discuss your plans for a wonderful future, a quiet life, a little house on the riverbank or in a distant village or a city square with lots of good books, handsome powerful dogs, a pony for riding and an old friend to come visiting on spring evenings? Every time she answered that I was the first. She told me she had never said "I love you" to anyone else ...'

Sindbad stroked the unhappy young man's hair. 'Come along, Milord. It's night. I know a friendly house nearby where the lady of the house is a wise old woman, an old sweetheart of mine, and so respectable you can tell her all your cares and woes. She has three young daughters of marriageable age. They usually make music in the evening and they sing and talk politics. Here you can forget your troubles a while, Milord. One of the daughters looks precisely as Mrs Boldogfalvi did in her youth.'

'But what about her soul?' sighed Albert.

'As pure as a child's!'

'Mrs Boldogfalvi's was far from pure, and it was just that I liked in her,' Albert replied and pulled his wide-brimmed hat down over his tear-filled eyes. Then clutching Sindbad's arm he left the dining room.

It was night: an owl sat on the dead sumach tree and the music had died away by the time a lone Sindbad ambled home down roads near the old church and in the light of the moon hiding behind the clouds The Bear resembled nothing so much as a chalet on a Swiss postcard.

'Lord,' thought Sindbad, 'give me untroubled dreams and a quiet night. Stop my ears against words poured into it by women. Help me forget the scent of their hair, the strange lightning of their eyes, the taste of their hands and the moist kisses of their mouths. Lord, you who are wise, advise me when they are lying, which is always. Remind me that the truth is something they never tell. That they never do love. Lord, up there, far beyond the tower, think occasionally of me, a poor, foolish man, an admirer of women, who believes in their smiles, their kisses, their tickling and their blessed lies. Lord, let me be a flower in that garden where lonely women retreat in the knowledge that no one's by. Let me be a lantern in the house of love where women mutter and babble and sigh the same old words. Let me be the handkerchief into which they weep their false tears. Lord, let me be just a gatepost ladies pass light-heartedly while clinging to the arms of their suitors.

Lord protect me, never let me fall into the hands of women.'

Having said this, his hand firmly and sincerely clasped to his heart, he entered The Bear with quiet, thoughtful steps and went to bed.

Shortly after this, Sindbad travelled up to Pest and sought out Mrs Boldogfalvi.

'I arranged things with Albert,' he told her as he settled himself in her room. The woman squeezed his hand in gratitude.

'My saviour! I was really frightened of that wild young man.'

'I have found him a post,' Sindbad went on. 'He won't trouble you again.'

Mrs Boldogfalvi stroked his cheek. 'Milord,' she trembled.

Sindbad shrugged. 'Madam, if you wish to enrol me among your worshipful admirers would you please invent some new name for me.'

Polly put her finger on her lip and nodded in agreement.

'My poor Albert,' Mrs Boldogfalvi said later. 'I wonder if he thinks of me.'

'I shouldn't think so,' answered Sindbad coldly. 'I have arranged a very nice house for him.'

'You are a wicked man, a devil!' cried Polly, frowning. 'And that is what I shall call you from now on.'

The Red Ox

The inn had a gate at the back which opened on to a winding side street where starving stray dogs waded through knee-high mud, sniffing at the rubbish. The gate seemed to be made expressly so that gypsy bands might cart their double basses and dulcimers through it at night, or so that penniless tramps could sneak through under cover of a winter fog at twilight and find somewhere to sleep beneath the straw in the stable. No one would have believed that this suspicious-looking gate, which, like many rural gates, was covered in red and white graffiti advertising the name of the second fiddle, and an incised heart commemorating the love of the stable lad for the barmaid, should serve as an entrance for women a little lower than princesses in rank, raising the dreamy frills of their skirts above their delicate shoes, clutching their hands to their hearts at the grotesque circumstances, their lips trembling under their veils as they passed the lamp-post where any night they might find some poor man stabbed through the heart, his lifeblood leaking away, all this so they could take a final farewell of Sindbad.

In those days Sindbad spent all his time at The Red Ox inn. He had gained some notoriety in town on account of a divorce which was settled amicably enough, and of one young lady, who had been determined to commit suicide on his account, then being despatched to a convent, though within a few years she had given birth to half a dozen beautiful children.

Having died and grown wise, he revisited The Red Ox in ghostly form, and found the vaulted room in which he had once hidden away utterly unchanged. The cupboard in the wall opened no more easily than it did then; some murdered tradesman might have been gripping it fast from within. A long shoehorn peeped out from under the bed like a watchful lapdog. The lamp hanging from the vaulted ceiling threw a sad light across the floor just as it did when it used to shine in the face of sleepless over-excited men counting the raindrops on the roof or warming a revolver under the pillow. Once upon a time lovers' eyes might have been drawn to the circle of light reflected on the limewashed wall; someone has left a window open in the house and the night wind is banging it bitterly against its jamb. The lock might have been stolen from a cell of the local monastery and down the cool brick-lined hallway one can already hear the uncertain approach of delicate feet. The kiss tastes of salt and tears and perfume, it is possibly the first yielded by some foreign princess to the man inside, the meeting at this mutually convenient staging post having been arranged in a correspondence comprised of long letters. Then they travelled on, by mail coach or by boat, one to the north, the other to the south, leaving nothing behind at The Red Ox except a forgotten hairpin which would later be found by another sleepless traveller who would turn it between his fingers and wonder about the history that lay behind it.

'Do you hear the wind moaning?' Sindbad asked himself one Sunday afternoon in winter as he settled in the room. The logs made such a row in the stove it seemed as if a troop of frozen wandering spirits had come to life in the snow-covered bark of the pine and were beating their fists against its walls.

The hall was haunted by the familiar smell of beer barrels and yesterday's paprika stew, a fact that did not go unremarked by hungry frost-bitten travellers as they trooped into breakfast, where they would stab at the meat with their pocket knives in evident gastronomic delight. Horses shook their bells in the yard as if preparing to set out for some Christmas Eve party a long way off; an old grey-haired, upper-class woman in a man's overcoat slurped at her spiced wine; and, as the unfamiliar bells of the church of the unfamiliar town rang for noon, the green walls of its storeyed tower glinted coquettishly in the sunlight, still competing for attention in its mad old age. The ringing usually began once the horn of the mail coach was heard, and the large yellow vehicle boomed and rattled over the stone bridge, down the snow-covered street with its tiny shops, whose owners rubbed their hands in the hope that the coach just now arriving might hold not merely the village schoolmistress or the notary in his green hat worn at a jaunty angle and his frock coat, together with other local officers in whose honour, on Wednesdays and Saturdays, The Red Ox provided freshly opened kegs of beer, but some long-desired, rich, potential customer.

As the mail coach passed the inn on its way down the clean street with its smell of monkshood, Sindbad glimpsed a tinder-coloured bonnet through the frost-scarred window, accompanied by the usual long wolfskin coat, grey officer's gloves and short boots. This was she, Francesca, who in her youth had danced through the winter balls with such conspicuous grace, and with whom Sindbad had spent so many delightful days staying in Number Seven, the corner room, whenever they came into town from the nearby village, when the snow came up to one's waist and the sounds of music rose up from under the balcony. Long ago, one winter night when the smell of hot punch blended with the scent of ball-dresses in the cold hall, when the girls' hair had come undone and was blowing like long grass in the wind and everyone was gently humming along with the bitter-sweet waltzes being played by the band, Francesca had been far kinder to Sindbad than the voyager deserved. She laid permanent claim to him that night during a brief absence from the hall, and an hour later, in the course of the quadrille, while Sindbad, who seemed to have reverted to adolescence, was still blethering on about eternal love, she stared at him coldly, angrily, almost malevolently. 'Leave me alone. Be off with you. I'm not in a good mood,' she said. Sindbad departed at dawn, his hot, aching head leaning against the darkest corner of the coach, leaving the music of the ball ever further behind him. A day or two later the wind would sweep one or two vestiges of that heavenly music into his memory. It was like being on a hilltop and hearing music in the brightly lit castle across the valley. Three knocks echoed from the room next door. At the sound of this prearranged signal Sindbad felt a mixture of anticipation and shyness, something he had always felt throughout his long life whenever he set out for a rendezvous.

'How white your hair is now!' exclaimed Francesca after she had taken full stock of Sindbad. 'There are long boring nights in the village when I put my feet up in front of the fire and try to conjure up a picture of you, but I can only manage your voice. There has only been one man since then with a voice like yours, a horse-dealer who tried to steal my cross-bred mare from me.'

Sindbad smiled sadly. 'I have never completely forgotten you.'

'You really should have given up lying by now, especially since I hear that liars are put in irons in your present abode in the afterlife.'

Her voice had become sharper and harder, and her look more commanding than it had been in her girlhood. Sooty-faced robbers might have broken in on her at night and she would calmly have shot them. The horses of her carriage might have bolted, throwing the driver, and she would have taken over the reins. Her children might have died in an epidemic and she would have cradled the head of a little corpse in her lap throughout the night.

Sindbad put the little flute he had been prepared to play for her back into its satchel. He addressed Francesca in a cold interrogatory manner. 'Did you never feel sick of life? Have you been happy or un-happy?'

'I have been both. Anyone who tries to arrange his life in one mode only is simply an ass. I have been in love, have loved and been loved, have given and received. I have done my crying. I woke to find it was morning, and was delighted to find cold fresh water in my bowl. The dew dripping from leaves helped me forget I had spent the night in the muck and sweat of a ball, that trembling hands had touched my waist and lustful kisses fluttered on the nape of my neck and that, like a fool, I had believed I had the finest head of hair in all Hungary. I have always loved cold water and cleanliness. I made my own soap as I made my own bed. That may be why I did not succumb to either melancholy or to happiness. I have all my own teeth, Sindbad. In fact, a new tooth appeared not so long ago. But you, you look as scruffy as a scarecrow in the snow,' said Francesca and stroked Sindbad's cheek. 'But I was never really angry … Only in a gentle, old womanish sort of way, when I couldn't remember what you looked like, however hard I tried.'

Sindbad nodded. 'If you had loved me I would have appeared. It doesn't matter now. Is there anything I can do for you? I have many good friends among the dead. Your house hasn't been troubled by unhappy wandering spirits?'

'The dead don't scare me, neither do the living. I am forty years old and for years now my greatest delight has been to see my pet animals frisking in the spring.'

'You used to like dancing and were moved by music. Tell me, don't you ever hear wind chimes in abandoned gardens?'

Francesca laughed softly. 'I enjoy a good stew with foaming light ale to accompany it. I like the strong red of crushed paprika, and wayside innkeepers tell me their troubles because I have a friendly face. Let's go out for dinner. It'll soon be evening and I'd like to be home in the village before dark.'

'Life,' thought Sindbad. 'Frivolous, holy, holy and wearisome life! How nice it would be to start again!'

Marabou

In the course of his long life Sindbad had spent many summers and winters in the company of that sad and noble gentlewoman, Irén Váraljai, and he tended to retreat to her friendly home in the village whenever he suffered some injury or disappointment, thinking in his bitterness to take farewell of Irén before committing suicide, for he had respected and honoured her for a decade and a half, so much so that he felt almost ridiculous that he should, after all that had happened, hold any woman in such high regard.

In her youth, Irén had danced in the first foursome of the Wiener Waltz at the opera. Her father – a retired Captain of Horse like an eccentric character from an English novel – would wait for her at the stage entrance and had credit with all the butchers along the usual route from home, even in the Krisztina district of Buda where they lived in a house with a sumach tree in the yard that was the first to hear the noonday peal of the nearby tower.

It was pure luck that Váraljai, who owned some village plots, a few provincial shares and a lot of old family pictures, found himself at the Pest opera one day and through the opera glasses he had inherited from his mother (the glass was missing from one tube) spotted Irén. Váraljai, the country landowner, might have been anything in the whirl of that strange Balkan capital – a horse-dealer, a cardsharp, a city slicker, or a terminally bankrupt petty nobleman from the sticks, spending his days watching old tradesmen playing cards in a café in one of the outer suburbs. But he was born under a lucky star – Sindbad adopted him as a friend as soon as he saw his passion for Irén. 'Why not make this ignorant and provincial young man happy, not to mention the sweet young lady whose ankles have been so appreciated by elders old enough to have spied on Susanna in the Bible?'

Soon enough an opportunity was found to introduce Váraljai to the Captain of Horse, and after performances the three of them would escort Irén home to her house in the sleepy Krisztina district, and returning at night Sindbad would invariably stop his friend from the country on Chain Bridge above the faintly murmuring river. Here, while the wandering scholar of heaven drew his yellow cloak across the waves, he would educate him in the arts of dreaming, chivalry and sensibility.

'Women are the only thing worth living for,' said Sindbad shortly before the churches of Buda tolled for midnight. 'A pity I am too old to begin my life anew.'

The retired Captain of Horse did not have to be taught to redouble his vigilance at the stage door and the innocent tulle skirt of the ballerina spun ever faster, ever more entrancingly. From behind the mysterious wings miraculous blinding lights flooded the auditorium and the loud orchestra cast nets of golden melody over the audience. Sindbad persuaded Váraljai to replace the missing lens in his opera glasses. One day, when wild chestnuts were blossoming in the Buda gardens, Váraljai felt an irresistible urge to confess his feelings.

The Captain's blond moustache bristled. 'Minor nobility from the sticks. Of course, I couldn't wish anything better for my daughter.'

Sindbad nodded in response and tried to pacify the old gentleman. 'The main thing, sir, is that your daughter should be happy. In marriage it is of no account whether a man hails from the country or the town. In any case we are all provincials.'

Soon enough two apparently happy people passed through the customs house of the capital after their marriage ceremonies were over. The retired Captain of Horse was apprehensive as he questioned Sindbad. 'What is there left for me to do? I have no one now. I am an orphan.'

'We shall sit and play dominoes in the coffee-house like all the other aged gentlemen,' answered the traveller and the Captain never saw him again.

A year had passed and Mr and Mrs Váraljai invited Sindbad to visit them. The traveller discovered warm friends and a splendid welcoming home in their village house. The dancer of the first foursome turned out to be an outstanding housewife; often it was she who went to milk the temperamental cow and she had already learned the language village women spoke to their domestic animals.

'I haven't even used your wedding present, Sindbad,' said Irén politely.

'I hope you will never have occasion to use it,' the traveller answered.

Sindbad had given Irén a marabou fan he had bought with an old countess's legacy. It was an enormous ceremonial-looking thing, the marabou feathers stately holding their position with a firm grace as if permanently expecting compliments of that rare and refined sort admirers might whisper into the ear of the fortunate lady wielding them, the proud feathers anticipating the excitement of a snatched kiss in the shadowy recesses of a private box at the opera and the pretence of wrestling with one's conscience before acquiescing, 'Tomorrow, five o'clock …' If an old marabou fan could speak it would have many confidences to betray, many ladies and gentlemen of days gone by to unmask. After all, it isn't so long since ladies of discretion employed the language of fans, a language now fallen out of use.

In this house by the river, among gently sloping hills of the village, where the evening clouds still moved to the rhetorical cadences of Kisfaludy's verse, Sindbad invariably found his corner room with its private entrance and its floor freshly scrubbed. A man might dream away a summer afternoon in the company of his sisters and mother here. Having narrowly escaped being ground under the heels of some heartless woman or avoiding some ill-fated meeting, he would pack his heart in his travelling bag and be on his way, while scheming women attempted to console him by recounting their own woes. 'Oh, my dear friend, I myself often weep when I'm alone,' they assured him. This house in the village was like a friend, selflessly waiting for Sindbad to appear. It was as if its affectionate atmosphere and quiet happiness represented his one worthy act, for the sake of which Sindbad's other, less worthy acts, might yet be overlooked.

Here, the traveller's eyes rested more readily on the leaves of the wild vine than on Irén's open-necked blouse. Whole years went by without him showing any curiosity as to the colour of Irén's slippers. And at supper he addressed himself to the gentle Váraljai rather than to her. 'No,' he said to the devil who on summer afternoons used to tempt him by parading in white sunlit dresses. 'I am not going to burden my conscience with this particular sin.' There was only one occasion, when Irén prepared a little pillow with yellow ribbons for Sindbad's special convenience and he discovered a long dark wisp of hair on it, and he could imagine that that afternoon, while he had been away, her head had rested and dreamt on it. In the deceptive light of dusk Sindbad thought he recognised it as Irén's and because of this he shortly left the hospitable house and only returned after a certain time had elapsed.

But Váraljai, like many good, gentle, sterling fellows, died young. Irén was shaken by his unexpected death. Already one care-worn line had spread itself across her brow, and now it lengthened and settled like a halo. Her childlike smile grew grave as if she had spent long sleepless nights staring into the darkness. Her expression, which for Sindbad had conjured the fresh scent of plum trees in spring, now brought to mind long autumn rains, evenings wrapped in shawls on the cool terrace in fading light and the aimless rattling of fallen leaves. He is a child sitting on a low stool, apprehensively, almost fearfully watching the garden yawning with autumn. His great aunt keeps a little yellow skull in the laundry cupboard. He is saying a hasty goodbye to a woman crying in a highland village, the night dark and the rain mournfully beating on the carriage roof.

He paid a few more visits after that. Irén would be decently occupied in knitting and the guest room was no longer freshly scrubbed. There were mice in the house and he could hear them running about the attic among the dried chestnuts. The sweet-scented bed smelled of old newspapers still bound up with string as they were when the subscriber first received them and put them aside. And every night the dry branch of the poplar scraped against the window of the guest room since there was no one in the house to prune it.

'Has another woman taken advantage of you?' asked Irén, the former dancer, her voice a little heavy. Like many old women in the village, she wiped her mouth with her fingers before she spoke.

Sindbad nodded sadly and felt rather sorry for himself. Fate might have made Irén young and beautiful or old and kind, someone who waited for him at the railway station, ready to welcome him with longed-for village pleasures and healthful airs. Irén turned over the knitting in her hand. 'Any man who places his trust in women is a fool, and you, dear sir, are the most foolish of all. Lie down and I'll massage your back because you don't look too steady on your feet.'

Later the ex-dancer prepared a herbal tea, had some leeches brought over from the chemist and Sindbad sweated through the night in his old friends' house under heavy village eiderdowns. Only once did he venture to ask the question he had always wanted to ask her – and that was after his death in his unquiet period – about that strand of hair on his pillow.

'Certainly not,' answered Irén sternly. 'I never kissed you in your sleep. Didn't you yourself tell me never to have recourse to the marabou fan?'

Madness from beyond the Grave

Sindbad spent some of his time as a ghost in a country graveyard because, having committed a sin or two in the neighbourhood, he was instructed to do penance there. The weeping willows and wooden monuments remembered him of the time he used to walk through the old cemetery with a provincial lady on his arm, their forms intertwined like twin stems in a single pot; they also recalled how he lied, continuously, fluently, without any let or hindrance, perpetually grinding out his insincerities like some busy watermill on the great River Danube. The old miller helpfully lifts the sacks of flour on to the narrow shoulders of willing maidens, a melancholy young man on the roof pipes a tune to the corpses of suicides clinging to the mill-wheel, the catfish glints in the moonlit stream like a medieval king in a silver cloak, and one old wild duck in the reeds informs another in the language of men that someone else has gone and killed himself for love. And in the old cemetery, where the traveller's mouth pours forth a constant stream of highly coloured words, strewing the lady's path with golden flour so that he may eventually load that flour into a precious silver sack which the poor woman will have to carry all her life till

her back breaks with the effort – there, in the old
cemetery where neither the worm-eaten wooden monuments, nor the rain-beaten, rust-furred gravestones that
look like strange dogs have ever succeeded in tripping
up a passing woman – there, the women walk beneath
weeping willows whose boughs the sylphs must part to
prevent the cold damp leaves brushing their naked
necks, for if the leaves did touch them it might possibly
destroy their illusions and prevent them journeying on
to joy and endless sorrow. 'On your way, on your way,'
mumble the old bones underground, yawning and
stretching in their coffins, while Sindbad's lies multiply
and multiply, covering the whole district with golden
dew, as far as the distant blue chain of mountains and
the desolate watchman's hut by the railway. Emma was
the name of the woman whom he had so mercilessly
abused. He had devoured her the way a starving red-
bearded bandit freed after twenty harsh years of captiv-
ity might devour the woodcutter's daughter in the forest.

Naturally enough, he spent most of his penitential
years at Emma's graveside. He sat hunched on the
mound, like an old crow on a cold autumnal day, tapping
the sealed tomb every so often: on particularly rainy
nights he could be heard howling miserably like the
siren of a distant ship.

'Can I help it if women are so gullible? Why are they
so quick to believe anything that is pleasant, delightful
and flattering to them? Those with hooked noses, weak
mouths, cold soulless eyes and wicked lying little souls,
why should they believe that they are made for love?
Poor women, learn from my wickedness never to yield

yourselves up except after a long and passionate siege, and spend some time each day washing your hearts in the waters of scepticism and forgetfulness; give not a single thought to the man who left you; nor waste your days weeping alone in darkened rooms, for tears are like fleet horses that gallop you to the grave.'

The ghost made such a pother at night that local lovers no longer dared visit the old graveyard. Over the years, though, long dead grandmothers had grown well used to the idea of their granddaughters responding to the first heart-rending sound of a man's voice, a voice that formed like mist across a silver mirror, directly above them. The cemetery had served as a trysting place for rich and poor alike – everyone in the little town had explored the hidden path by the ditch that ran through it. Others sleeping in the ditch included tiny souls who had perished downless, featherless, in their embryo state or at nest-robbing time, as exiles from the wonder and brilliance of life. They slept on quietly under the snow while their mothers were dancing and whirling their skirts at The Bugle Boy nearby, though sometimes, on a wet spring day, they took the form of little frogs and hopped onto their mothers' feet as they were crossing the ditch again.

The continual crying of this restless spirit in the graveyard frightened off prospective lovers. There were no more visitors, their fingers intertwined like the topmost branches of young poplars, their warm thoughts full of life and darting about the air like swallows, who might stop to meditate on wooden monuments whose inscriptions proclaimed the longevity of old women.

The dead woman lay unmoving in her grave: having committed suicide, she was forbidden the pleasures of love in the nether world. Vainly did Sindbad's midnight tears seep through the holes where beetles had burrowed. 'Tell me, tell me, how could you be so stupid as to believe me?'

One day, the daughter of the dead woman came to visit her grave. The sight of Emma's daughter so disturbed the ghost, who had been sleeping among the leaves in the trees, that the heart which long ago had died in him gave a great leap. A moment later he was informing the sexton that according to the contract made on the day he died he was entitled to one single occasion of awaking. The sexton looked up the contract and in a few minutes a melancholy, dark-haired student in a velvet jacket appeared under the weeping willows, treading his way towards Emma's daughter who was just then gathering dry leaves from the grave.

An old graveyard bat stirred in his daytime sleep and said to the owl: 'The suicide's beautiful daughter is here. She has swallowed a gold ring and the student is about to cut her heart open to retrieve it. It's the ring he gave her mother.'

'Serve people right,' answered the owl. 'Why should they always be thinking of yesterday! People spend their whole lives discussing what has already happened.'

In the meantime the student had introduced himself to Emma's daughter and was speaking in lightly flavoured violet-scented words of her mother – who was probably terrified and sitting up in her coffin.

'Oh, my mother,' said Emma's daughter. 'Night after night she comes and sits at my bedside with her hair glowing like silver letters on the black ribbon tied around a wreath. Yet she was dark-haired, brown as I am now, at the time she died.'

'And are you happy?' asked Sindbad, without preamble, since it was already getting on to evening.

'I have learned by my mother's example. I keep happiness at arm's length, lock my heart into my prayer-book and, thank God, have had no occasion for praying yet. I am twenty years old and teach in a school.'

'Yet nature tells us ...' Sindbad began, then suddenly fell quiet as if ashamed in the presence of those ancient wooden monuments which seemed to be leaning forward, listening intently, though they had heard it all before and in much the same words too.

'I have lived a very long time,' he said glumly. 'There are whole volumes that could be written about me. Old gentlemen in their dotage might read them, wagging their incredulous heads; feeble old countesses might admonish the young attendant appointed to entertain them for sullying their ears with such wickedness. I can imagine people using my name to frighten naughty children on stormy nights, that is, if they had any notion who I was ... All I can tell you, young lady, is that love was the only thing worth persevering for, weeping for and living for. The sparkling jewels you wear in your hair will one day adorn some other woman's breast like props in a play; by the time you are old the delicate silks which now cover your body might serve to polish the shoes of the local Madame Bovary before she goes out to commit adultery; the song you were singing with such passion by the lake will have sunk under the waves like a virtuous urchin and a greedy pike will be nibbling at it. Love alone remains as a low, bitter, ever-restless memory, with the scent of hours which are nothing but memories. Some nights I hear voices that seem to portend something, whether good or ill I cannot tell, sighs which seem to contain my whole life. The love which first entered your heart in the guise of some groom's best-man or as a suitor in clinking spurs, or like a shy melancholy wanderer, that love remains with you for ever. The waves cannot swallow such memories, the wind cannot blow them away. They are yours alone. What you have loved remains yours: all that caused you unhappiness, that for which you cried in your pillow, for which you died ... I am in love with you, dear lady.'

The graveyard owl repeated his previous observation. 'People will go wittering on about the past.'

By now it was evening, the moon was peeking through the branches like an officious warden and Emma's daughter, standing by her mother's grave, suddenly noticed that the student had gone from her side, his leave of absence having expired, and that her hand which had been in another's warm grip a moment ago was now cold and empty. Her hungry ears heard only the whispering of the wind.

The woman who had killed herself spoke quietly from the tomb, her voice as soft as the rain on the leaves. 'Go home and do as Sindbad advised. The man is right.'

Escape from Life

'**O**nce spring comes we'll go out to the country,'
Mrs Bánatvári used to say on early winter evenings as she strolled arm in arm with Sindbad
down Hat Street. 'We have decent horses, a fine coach,
faithful servants and a nice country house. After all,
what is mine is yours.'

Sindbad clung happily to the widow's arm. 'I have
always fancied being a country landowner, galloping
through the countryside in my carriage, learning the
local dialect, waiting with frost-nipped cheeks on a cold
morning at the local station for the passenger train to
arrive, a weekly market at the cathedral town nearby,
and a casino for the gentry where one could stop for a
glass of beer, a bit of local politics and good general
gossip. How delightful it would be to live without care,
to sleep long and deep with dreams that move like slow
lumbering barges and to rise with the sun, fresh and
ready for the new day!'

'I'll take you with me,' Mrs Bánatvári answered, her
voice trembling with emotion. 'You'll see how the old
women kiss my hand. I am godmother to all the local
infants and the men still remember my grandfather
leading them in his red beret at the time of the revolu-

tion. There is an apiary where you can fall asleep and dream to your heart's content and Uncle Samu inevitably turns up in the afternoon for his game of cards and funny stories. Or, if you prefer, you can go to the Grozinger and play bowls with the others, and my finances will even allow you to treat the local dignitaries to a daily barrel of beer. You must watch out for the miserly clerk and offer the mean fellow his daily cigar. You must praise the singing of the schoolmistress and speak approvingly of the chickens the minister's wife likes to keep. Futray need to be supplied with a few piquant stories and when you speak with the young ladies be sure to mention how you danced with their mothers at the local ball and how they were such great flirts.'

'I will accept your advice in all these matters, my guardian angel,' Sindbad answered resolutely, with all the gratitude of one escaped from a shipwreck, for secretly he had been sobbing through his dreams every night on account of some woman's wicked demeanour. He stopped suddenly in the middle of the street, his head bent, and paying no attention to the traffic rushing past him, wandered over to a shop window hardly noticing the goods on view. He stumbled down streets he had never seen before and was content to lose his way among unfamiliar houses. He imagined himself wandering aimlessly in a foreign city, bundles of unopened mail waiting for him at the hotel. He couldn't bear to pronounce the woman's name because the effort cost him such physical pain it flooded through him from head to foot so that the thermometer beneath his arm showed a distinct rise, and whenever he found himself alone and took out her picture it was such delicious agony he had to rest his head on his arm. 'How marvellous it was to love her,' he wrote on a scrap of paper then dropped it into the Danube. He straightened his back, his eyes flashed, and an idiotic excitement drove his heart forward like the sails of a mill whenever he saw someone who from the back reminded him of her. The woman's name was 'F.' or that, at least, is how he now thought of her, having sworn to Mrs Bánatvári never to pronounce the other letters of her name. F. He carefully examined every letter F he saw in the street, on shop signs or on soldier's buttons, it was all the same to him. On pâtisseries and fashion stores, the delicate *f* brought to mind her supple waist; the royal monogram *'FJ'* which the head gardener had sown in tulips near the central balcony of the state gardens invariably reminded him of the slender legs she so frequently displayed. 'I'm sure to commit suicide in the country,' thought Sindbad as Mrs Bánatvári led him in motherly manner through the streets of the city centre.

By now they were counting the days before leaving the capital. 'And think of all those ugly people who envy us our happiness,' added Mrs Bánatvári. All those little objects she so superstitiously collected, those portraits of pale-faced, frock-coated, wavy-haired gentlemen painted on ivory, whom Mrs Bánatvári would have fallen in love with had she lived at the time the pictures were painted, all those books on the bedside table, all were transferred into her travelling bag; Petőfi's* poems together with those of Aladár Benedek* (since she read no poetry after Benedek), the heavy Egyptian *Book of Dreams,* a volume of *Carthusian Meditations,** the *Book of Card Games* which was required reading in the country where the local intelligentsia slap the table when play grows exciting and lastly, a human skull. All these would accompany them on their journey.

'Oh, and I mustn't forget my pistol,' muttered Mrs Bánatvári in that voice so frequently adopted by faint, expensive, dreamy women. 'You are my last love, Sindbad, and life won't be worth living if you leave me.'

Sindbad, who watched these preparations with his hands tucked deep into his pockets as if these great yawning suitcases with their pink labels bearing the names of hotels in foreign capitals were nothing to do with him, was thinking that he would appropriate Mrs Bánatvári's little pistol and not go to the country house after all. There was a golden box he noticed before it went into the suitcase. It contained a letter torn into tiny shreds.

'That was written in farewell by the man who loved me most of all,' Mrs Bánatvári whispered and crossed herself.

'We'll read it once we're in the country,' Sindbad muttered.

Here were strange little mirrors which must once have shown the lady in the full bloom of her beauty, shreds of lace, plumes from hats, the sewing needles that accompany women wherever they go, various rings a superstitious creature might collect in the course of her life, rings to guard her against disease, cataracts, drowning, all kinds of misfortune, rings to ward off hopeless love and sleepless nights, all strung on a silk thread. There was a range of buttons suitable for coats and dresses and a collection of little scissors each of which might have been christened with a name of its own, and an altar-cloth she had begun to embroider some twenty years ago and which she still took out every summer. There was the history of the Count of Monte Cristo and a silver flask intended to store tea or water for boiling. Into the case with them all. Mrs Bánatvári had a kind word for each of them, each conjured some pleasant memory. But she did not forget about Sindbad either.

'Some time in the summer we'll have to pay a visit to that little Polish spa where a sick gentleman once carved a statuette of the Virgin for me … We'll go simply everywhere, just as we did with my first husband who was an inveterate traveller. Switzerland, Italy – everywhere he called the hotel porters by name. He knew the best inns in every town, local fashions, local idioms … Sindbad, you will escape to the good life with me, into life as it should be lived.'

Sindbad smiled and nodded, wondering whether F knew he was leaving the capital for ever.

'We'll spend two of the summer months in the village. I'll talk to the lime trees, the horses and the cows, for I'm a sentimental sort of woman,' she continued dreamily. 'There's a chimney there that will mumble, indeed practically talk, only when I spend a night under the roof. We have a feral cat that runs about in the forest with others of its kind but it senses my presence and returns to the house when I am at home. My grandfather's old horse, a forlorn-looking creature, tosses his head restlessly when the train carrying me blows its whistle at the station, and as for the servants and old women, they dream long convoluted dreams in my honour, and it is my task to explain these to them. Rooms long shut up are bathed in sunlight and dusty old mirrors used only by ghosts in my absence grow young again. I cure the diseased trees and the swallow in the eaves recognises me. Do you like the sound of it, Sindbad?'

Sindbad nodded enthusiastically. 'It all sounds very fine,' he sighed, completely surrendering himself to the idea, as if he could already see himself swimming in the river, staring into the sun with sightless eyes while the fish engaged him in conversation, enquiring about the latest fashions. Was it truly the end of that marvellous life he had lived at F's side? From this day on he would be an elegant country gentleman, companion to a sweet, dreamy, superstitious woman with a voice like old sheet music, who, none the less, could not screw her eyes up half so charmingly as that other one whose voice had a more animal quality, whose laughter bubbled, who did not call Sindbad to the enjoyments of a quiet life, but rather to death, decay and annihilation, to the dance to exhaustion at the ball of life where the masked guests are encouraged to lie, cheat and steal, to push old people aside, to mislead the inexperienced young, and always to lie and weep alone ...

'We have a little church whose foundation I have decided to endow in my will, the church where everyone has learned to pray. Do not forget this foundation,

Sindbad, for since I have met you I have changed my will. Everything is yours, and it is a pretty sum.'

Sindbad turned his head away and thought how nice it would be to present that pretty sum to the other, to deposit the whole amount in an envelope and slip it into her hand then run away.

'Together we will visit the grave of my poor uncle,' said Mrs Bánatvári as she sat on the trunk. 'You are fond of the old gentleman, aren't you? He has such a kind and gentle face in those old pictures. And how fond he was of me! He forgave me everything and never pulled my hair but stroked it instead.'

'I am very fond of the old gentleman,' trembled Sindbad and felt as though he was choking. 'I'll be back in a minute.'

He quietly slid from the room. At the door he cast a timid glance back. Mrs Bánatvári stood in the middle of the room in her travelling coat and little veiled hat, her eyes wide with an expression of terror, her arm half raised as if seeking the hand of an angel above her. Her nose had reddened like a tearful child's and a strange sobbing welled from deep in her breast.

Sindbad ran down the stairs. Once in the street he broke into a crazy laugh. He escaped people's attention by sheltering in a dark doorway. He leaned his head against the wall and repeated loudly and often, 'Fanny!'

Escape from Death

Omne night he found Fanny under a lamp-post in a square in Buda. She was wandering aimlessly, her head bowed, a heavy veil drawn over her face. She was wearing an expensive dress and carrying an aristocratic parasol in her hand. A mild-faced policeman with a blond moustache was treading warily beside her, speaking quietly and respectfully to her.

'Please, your ladyship, don't do it … People who try suicide invariably regret it. In any case the fishermen will soon pull you out, stretch you out on the bank, and the next day the papers will report it and all your innocent relatives will feel humiliated. Dear lady, I beg you, come with me and I will escort you to your house keeping a respectable distance.'

It was as if Fanny had not heard him at all. She continued on her way, her eyes fixed on the ground, seeking the Danube perhaps, or the railway cuttings; possibly she was not even thinking of death.

Sindbad touched her arm. 'Where are you going, Fanny?'

The woman raised her head, startled, then began to laugh loudly, strangely, with a touch of madness. 'I knew I would find you!' she said with the fanatical conviction of which women are capable.

'Look, it's my husband, my friend, my lover,' she turned to the policeman, speaking so loudly the windows shook in the sleeping, long silent square. 'You can put your mind at rest now, constable. I am not going to jump into the Danube.'

The policeman gestured discreetly to Sindbad that it would be best to keep an eye on the lady because something wasn't right, then he watched as the couple walked off arm in arm.

'Why are you on the street in the middle of the night?' asked Sindbad at the third crossing.

The woman gripped his arm very tightly as if fearing to lose him again. 'No ...' she said, as if in answer to some private thought. 'It was all a misunderstanding. We shall never leave each other again. That's right, isn't it? We shall never leave each other again?'

Her tears flowed like warm rain on a freshly ploughed field. They almost sang, as sometimes one hears the dawn rain sing in a lonely house, knowing that trees, bushes and roofs will soon be putting on their clothes of freshness and light.

'We shall never part again,' answered Sindbad. 'I have thought of nothing but you.'

'You know what I did?' the woman laughed. 'I stared at your picture, I dandled it on my knee as if you were my child and I talked to you, played with you; I laughed and cried as I did that first winter after my little son died. You were in the graveyard too, weren't you, and that's where you've come back from because I had need of you?'

'I've been on a long journey,' Sindbad answered quietly. 'Sometimes I thought I would never return.'

'But you see! I knew. I knew you would come back,' she laughed, raising her head as a little bird might. 'My pillows told me so at night, the trees under my window whispered it, as did my own lips when I prayed ... And tonight, when I was alone, walking up and down aimlessly, my hands linked, I stopped before the picture of my dead parents and my dear mother was suddenly speaking to me so clearly anyone might have heard her, saying, "You will see him!" I fell to my knees and wept before her picture. When everyone had abandoned me, when I was as low as I had ever been and thought my life was over, all laughter, all love, all my beauty done with, my mother stretched her hand out to me. "You will see him!" her voice rang out and suddenly my heart was full of lilacs bursting forth as they do at the feet of saints in country churches. I decided to put on my finest dress, the finest and most expensive, the one I had made for me when I first met you. I so wanted to look beautiful. I wanted to be the most beautiful woman you had ever seen, the most graceful, the most desirable. My maid was away so I dressed alone, skilfully, feeling an extraordinary happiness. Then I pricked my finger on a pin. My blood bubbled up and I would have been happy to bleed to death thinking I was dressing myself for you.'

'Child,' mumbled Sindbad, though, unquestionably, he felt rather flattered by her madness.

'And when I was dressed, when I stood before my mirrors to check that everything was as it should be, I left the house, stealthily as if escaping from something. Perhaps I would never go back – if I failed to find you and talk to you, if you didn't exhort me to live on for your sake, for your heart's sake, for your delight in me, your love of me ... if I did not hear in your voice the scent of leaves at first light, if I did not feel in your hand the gripping power of dreams, if I did not see in your eyes the rising sun as it sends brilliant white gulls scuttling into the heavy clouds that drift above the cold, austere waves of the lake at night.

'I set out as if I knew for certain my way would lead to you. I wondered through the twilit streets without any thought of where I was going, as I did when my child died and those kind passers-by dragged him from under the wheels of the carriage. I could see my own feet walking as if I were following myself in the failing light and people were asking themselves who was this poor woman with the bowed head and where was she going? A bright-eyed woman stared at me from a shop window, her face flushed as if in theatrical limelight. It's summer, she must have been thinking, the opera season is over, where is this strange woman going in full evening dress?

'Forgive me, Sindbad, for dwelling so long on externals. We women, all of us from the cleverest to the most stupid, are equally preoccupied with our appearance. You have no idea how ashamed I was that I could be thinking of the plume in my hat at the same time as my whole wonderful life, with all its youth, femininity, ambition and hopes was set to collapse or resurrect in front of me, then as I left to find you, wherever and however far I had to go.

'I walked down unfamiliar streets, passing houses I had never seen before, assailed by unfamiliar smells. Strange women dawdled past me, with wicked, calculating looks in their eyes.

'Some instinct drove me towards the Danube and I felt lighter at heart. I came to the bridge and crossed it perfectly calmly, thinking of nothing, nothing at all. I never imagined strange men might accost me – a person is not accosted if they behave reasonably – or that I might be attacked by some thief such as you read about in the papers – if they did I would simply hand over my jewels and walk on.

'How long did I continue walking? I no longer remember when I set out, the minutes are all mixed up like grains of sand. I saw a little inn with a green fence and a garden and a lantern hung on a post in the middle of it as in the penny dreadfuls, and dark-faced men were leaning together, pointing at me. I was not frightened, I did not tremble, and it was only some stupid sense of embarrassment that prevented me from going into the inn and ordering a glass of beer like cabmen do. Perhaps I thought they might not want to serve a woman alone, so I went on, heavy-hearted.

'Suddenly someone spoke to me. He coughed respectfully, speaking in a low voice. It was a policeman who asked me not to kill myself because I could lead a very happy life … "Happy, happy, happy!" my heart leapt, because I could sense you approaching, somewhere I heard your footsteps as I had heard them so often on quiet nights under my window; your face, with its bold open gaze, emerges from the shadows and I hear your fastidious voice ...'

Sindbad had never before listened so intently to a woman as he did then to Fanny. This black-haired, black-eyed, long-legged woman had filled his life and occupied his heart for more than a year and a half. And in that year and a half he would love to have caught her at some lie. He felt that somehow, in some way, Fanny wasn't telling him the truth, only he didn't know where the simple meadow of truth stopped and the brightly coloured field of lies began. 'Ah, but women are always lying,' he thought as he kissed away her tears and felt her fingers running through his hair, aware of the perfume lingering on his moustache as they walked home. He clung to the lamp-posts and stared into the air in front of him. Where precisely did the lies start?

They were passing the church in the High Street. 'Would you like me to swear, here, on the steps of the church, that I will never leave you again?' asked Sindbad, gazing into the woman's eyes.

'I know now that you will not desert me,' she answered with peculiar certainty and smiled at Sindbad. 'Tonight we shall die together.'

'We shall die,' Sindbad repeated mechanically.

'When you were deeply in love with me, when I was everything to you, when you knelt at my feet and we spent whole days crying or laughing together, or walked hand in hand and knew each other's thoughts without having to say them and gazed at each other happily, with unwearied love ... when our time fled by free as a bird, when we invented wholly new words of endearment to make each other happy, when we exchanged kisses that seemed to go on for ever, and when, behaving perfectly conventionally, we believed we were the chosen, the only pair of lovers, children of God, souls born in the moon and the sun, that was when you promised me we should die together.'

'Die together?' asked Sindbad, more of himself than of Fanny. 'I know death. Death is for women.'

'Come back with me. I've sent the servants away and I want to take farewell of my mother's picture. Calmly, with full premeditation, you will kill me, so that I can be looking at you as I die, until the moment I close my eyes and feel your lips on my brow, your hand holding my hand as we set out on the great journey. I am quite sure you will follow me, that you would not leave me alone in that vast unknown.'

'I will follow you,' Sindbad's voice trembled.

'If we were to stay alive we'd only part again. We'd weep and moan for each other, we would suffer exceedingly, and who knows whether we would love one another as deeply if we were to meet again.'

The man bowed his head. 'Love,' he sighed, like an exhausted gambler on his way home, having lost everything.

'We shall die, Sindbad. Together, happily, our hearts filled to overflowing. Who cares whether the sun rises in the morning. We will no longer care about the dawn.'

'It's dawn now.'

The woman shuddered. Girls on their way home from the other world were trailing grey veils across the

Danube. A seagull, like a wandering spirit, flew off bitterly in the direction of Pest having witnessed the last rites of darkness.

'It's dawn,' the woman repeated sadly, 'and once day comes I will no longer be able to die. The milkman is due, my husband will arrive by the first train, the servants will be up and ready to go to the market, the postman will deliver an invitation from a friend saying they intend to spend summer in the country and I shall go to hospital to visit my sick brother. Another time, Sindbad ... Should we meet again another night ...'

Fanny found a cab and waved Sindbad a resigned farewell. The cab slowly disappeared around the corner.

Sindbad took a deep breath. 'Heavens,' he thought, 'Mrs Bánatvári is still sitting on her trunk waiting for me.' He started to run and arrived at the doors of the house in Hat Street sweating and out of breath.

The woman was sitting on her trunk. 'I knew you would come back to me,' she said simply.

Sindbad collapsed onto the settee and before falling asleep smiled sweetly and gently, reflecting on how women were so sure of everything.

Notes

Page 1 – *Who he was*: the Lubomirskis were Polish princes and landowners whose property in Hungary included Podolin, which is itself now part of Slovakia. In the early seventeenth century Jerzy (George) Lubomirski set up various charitable foundations.

Page 16 – *sumach trees:* the sumach is a shrub or small tree of the genus *Rhus*. Certain kinds of sumach are indigenous to southern Europe and are used in the tanning process.

Page 21 – *Kaiser Baths*: the *Császár fürdő*. Many of the baths of Budapest are a legacy of the Ottoman occupation of the sixteenth and seventeenth centuries. The Kaiser Baths in Buda comprised Turkish baths and steam chambers. They are still open and in use today.

Page 27 – *Fisherman's Bastion:* The Fisherman's Bastion or *Halászbástya* is the mock-Romanesque fortress constructed betwen 1890–1905 on the hill top next to the Royal Palace overlooking the Danube. It provides romantic walks and panoramic views across the river.

Page 45 – *the guard dog is called Tisza, after the river:* the Tisza, 'the slothful Hungarian Nile' according to the nineteenth-century novelist Kálmán Mikszáth, is one of the two great rivers of Hungary. It runs through central and southern Hungary and joins the Danube between Novi Sad and Belgrade.

Page 47 – *tarlatan:* thin stiff muslin.

Page 55 – *Eperjes:* now Prešov in Slovakia, but in Krúdy's time it was the capital town of Sáros county in Hungary.

Page 60 – *the Great Bercsényi inn*: Count László Bercsényi (1689–1778), Marshal of France, was born in Eperjes. He founded the French Hussars. His father, Miklós, before him had been one of the most influential generals in Ferenc Rákóczi II's army. Rákóczi (1676–1735), Prince of Transylvania, led ultimately unsuccessful wars of liberation against the Austrians. His grave has long been an object of pilgrimage for Hungarians.

Page 63 – *Pancsova:* a town in Greater Hungary, now part of Yugoslavia, some ten miles from Belgrade, scene of Austrian victory over the Turks in 1739, and over the Hungarians in 1849.

Page 68 – *blue-dye man:* blue-dyeing is a traditional peasant craft and provides the basic colour for skirts, headscarves and other items of clothing.

Notes

Page 69 – *the White Woman of Lőcse:* Mór Jókai's novel, *A lőcsei fehérasszony* ('The White Woman of Lőcse') appeared in 1885. It is about the end of the Rákóczi campaign (see note to p. 60) in 1711. The central character is based upon the historical figure of Julianna Géczy, who betrayed the town of Lőcse, now in Slovakia, to the Austrians, and was consequently tortured and beheaded. A painting of her as a woman dressed in white was displayed at the town gates.

Page 74 – *half-crazed Jewesses:* Krúdy himself married a Jewish woman (see Introduction), and he wrote a defence of Jews accused of blood crimes.

Page 81 – *Kisfaludy:* Károly Kisfaludy (1788–1830) was the younger brother of the poet Sándor Kisfaludy (1772–1844). He wrote melodramatic plays and comedies as well as short stories and lyric poetry. His short stories focus on romantic subjects, but incorporate satirical elements.

Page 82 – *Liska:* pet form of Julia or Juliska.

Page 86 – *The body of St Ladislas being carried on a wagon:* St Ladislas, King of Hungary from c. 1040–95, founded bishoprics and was a hero of the wars against the pagans. He was canonised in 1192.

Page 86 – *the Matthias Church:* the Church of the Blessed Virgin in Buda. One of Hungary's most important and illustrious kings, King Matthias Corvinus (ruled 1458–90), was married here. In 1896 it was restored by Frigyes Schulek.

Page 86 – *King Béla:* King Béla III (1148–96) ruled Hungary from 1172 to his death. His remains were brought to the Matthias Church in 1848.

Page 90 – *Baron Miklós Jósika:* Baron Miklós Jósika (1794–1865), Transylvanian author, was regarded as the founder of the historical novel in Hungary, also its foremost theorist.

Page 97 – *Euphrosyne:* Krúdy calls her Fruzsina, the Hungarian equivalent. The name was popular in the eighteenth century.

Page 106 – *Kisfaludy:* see note to p. 81. Could be either of the brothers, possibly the elder.

Page 110 – *the Tabán district:* The Tabán, now mostly demolished for reasons of hygiene, was one of the oldest districts on the Buda side of the Danube, full of inns and restaurants.

Page 120 – *Aranykéz Street: Aranykéz utca*, means literally 'Goldenhand Street'. A street in Budapest.

Page 188 – *Petőfi:* Sándor Petőfi (1823–49) is Hungary's national Romantic poet in much the same way as Burns is Scotland's and was born at Kiskőrös in the

Hungarian Lowlands. His songs, ballads, sketches of village life and revolutionary lyrics are central to the Hungarian consciousness. It was his recitation of the *Nemzeti Dal* (National Song) from the steps of the National Museum that is thought to have sparked the 1848 revolution. He is traditionally supposed to have been killed in battle against the Russians at Segesvár (now Sighisoara, Romania), but his body was never found and some think that he might have been captured by the Russians and died in exile in Siberia.

Page 188 – *Aladár Benedek:* poet and editor, born in 1843, made his name in the 1860s and 1870s. An oppositional figure, he was the subject of official criticism which eventually silenced him. He died in 1915.

Page 189 – *Carthusian Meditations:* Baron József Eötvös's novel *A Karthauzi* (1839) ('The Carthusian') is set in France. The disappointed hero joins the Carthusian order.

TITLES IN SERIES

For a complete list of titles, visit www.nyrb.com or write to:
Catalog Requests, NYRB, 435 Hudson Street, New York, NY 10014